---------- ★ ----------

Footsteps sounded behind me.

Instinctively I ducked, and a sharp blow struck the back of my shoulder. I hit the wet concrete and rolled through the standing water to my right, out of the glare of the headlights into the darkness. The footsteps hurried toward me. Still on my back, I kicked out with my feet and slammed into someone's knees.

There was a grunt and a curse. A body bounced off the fender of my truck. I rolled to my feet just in time to see my assailant lift his arm once again. I did what any all-American boy would do. I kicked him where it hurt most.

He froze in midswing. A groan of agony hissed through his lips just before I slammed a knotted fist into the blur that was his face. I felt something give, and when he staggered backward, a dark film covered his chin. I hoped I'd busted his nose.

In the next instant he spun and, still holding himself, waddled to the edge of the wharf and leaped into the darkness.

---------- ★ ----------

GALVESTON

KENT
CONWELL

W🌐RLDWIDE®

TORONTO • NEW YORK • LONDON
AMSTERDAM • PARIS • SYDNEY • HAMBURG
STOCKHOLM • ATHENS • TOKYO • MILAN
MADRID • WARSAW • BUDAPEST • AUCKLAND

GALVESTON

A Worldwide Mystery/July 2013

First published by Avalon Books.

ISBN-13: 978-0-373-26854-2

Copyright © 2013 by Kent Conwell

Printed in U.S.A.

To Amy and Susan,
who kept going even when the going got tough.
And to my wife, Gayle. How she tolerates me,
I'll never know.

ONE

I WAS REARED in the bayous and sloughs of Louisiana, so, on occasion, I have had to study a moment on the proper fork at a formal dinner. But that doesn't mean I'm a naive bumpkin who believes the perfect means to ensure an unforgettable evening is to kill a cop. Especially if he is the cop I had once threatened in front of witnesses.

But, that's what everybody thought.

And the truth was, I didn't know if I could prove them wrong.

I'D BEEN OUT strolling a deserted wharf that night with Ben Howard, former Austin P.D. detective. I suppose another person might shiver at a sprawling, empty wharf enveloped in a thick layer of fog. Certainly the hollow click of heels on concrete, the mercury lights that were ghostly dots in the thick moisture, and the moaning fog-horns echoing across the bay added to the ghostly ambience of the night.

For me, it was a pleasant walk. Nothing ghostly, nothing spooky, nothing at all.

You want to talk spooky, then you pole a pirogue through the Atchafalaya Swamp during the dark of the moon and listen to the gurgle of water displaced by the alligators swimming alongside and the rustle of leaves in the overhanging limbs as snakes prowl for their next meal.

That's spooky. Not only spooky, it's scary.

Why Ben chose the Galveston docks for an after-dinner stroll, I had no idea. But I was his guest, and my mother brought me up to respect the wishes of my host. Personally, I would have chosen the bright lights and gay laughter of the Strand, Galveston's answer to New Orleans' Bourbon Street and Austin's Sixth Street.

The muffled rumble of an engine and the clashing of gears cut through the thick silence. I shrugged deeper into my jacket and peered into the fog. The shadowy phantom of a concrete truck emerged from the fog and drove past us.

Ben Howard grunted. "Late to be pouring cement."

"Yeah." I glanced in the direction from which the truck had come, expecting to see the diffused glare of construction lights. All I saw was more fog.

We continued our aimless strolling, bantering over the old days back in Austin. A few minutes later, we spotted the fuzzy outlines of two towering shore cranes silhouetted against the diffused glow of lights. They looked like hulking buzzards.

Beyond came the faint clatter of metal against concrete and a few muffled voices. A couple of shadows appeared, and then the sound of running feet faded into the fog.

"Somebody else working late," Ben muttered.

Before I could reply, four shots rang out, their reports muffled by the fog. I glimpsed the four bursts of orange beside one of the cranes.

Ben grunted, jerked backward, and spun to the ground. "Christ! What the…?"

I dropped to my knees beside him, then glanced toward the direction of the shots. A shadowy figure raced through the fog toward us.

Muttering a curse for leaving my .38 in my motel room, I jammed my hand inside Ben's coat for his service revolver.

Two more shots broke the foggy silence. A slug ricocheted off the concrete at my feet. I swung Ben's Smith & Wesson around at the charging figure and pulled the trigger.

Nothing.

I cursed again, remembering he preferred a single action. Hurriedly, I thumbed back the hammer and fired. In the next few seconds, I sent three more slugs into our assailant. The 240-grain slugs spun him around and sent him reeling to the wet concrete.

Keeping the revolver trained on the dark figure sprawled on the concrete, I nudged him with my toe. He rolled over, and his arms flopped out to his side. His eyes stared unseeing into the thickening fog. I frowned. He looked familiar. I bent over, my heart thudding against my chest. My eyes bulged.

Frank Cheshire.

I closed my eyes and shook my head. Frank Cheshire.

It couldn't be. Frank Cheshire. The cop I had sworn to kill.

A moan from Ben jerked me from my daze.

I knelt at the detective's side.

He coughed and looked up at me. "I shoulda known… known better than go anyplace with you, Boudreaux. You was always bad luck." A spasm of coughs racked his body. Blood, black as death under the ghostly street-lights, dribbled from the side of his lips, and he went limp.

Running steps sounded through the fog.

I shouted. "Call an ambulance! Two guys have been shot."

As the footsteps faded in the distance, I looked down at Ben Howard. For a moment, I considered getting the blazes out of there. I shifted my gaze to Frank Cheshire. If I had to shoot someone, why did it have to be the only cop I'd threatened to kill in front of witnesses? It had been long ago, but cops never forget.

I felt Ben's carotid artery. His pulse was strong. I did my best to plug up the leaking holes in him, and then I sat at his side on the wet concrete and waited for the inevitable.

Not once did I think that I might lose my newly earned private security license. Not once did I think I might be indicted for murder. Not once did I think I might have to arrest the black sheep cousin of my significant other back in Austin.

Not once!

TWO

THE LOCAL UNIFORMS were enraged. One of their own had been wounded, and another had been gunned down. They grilled me mercilessly, but after a few hours, they sent me back to my motel with orders to not leave the island.

EARLIER, I HAD met Ben at the police station and ridden with him down to Gui Lee's Steak and Pizza Emporium on the Strand, so my old pickup was in the parking lot at the station.

I swung by the hospital. Ben had just been moved from emergency. For the moment, he was stable. I breathed a sigh of relief. "Thanks," I told the ER nurse. "I'll check back in the morning."

A cruiser followed me all the way back to the motel. I brushed it off to police routine.

I slept in snatches, unanswered questions tumbling through my head. What was Frank Cheshire doing on the wharf so late at night? And why did he try to kill us? Or was it all a mistake?

OVER THE YEARS, I have become a great believer in happenstance, that quirk of fate that puts you where you don't want to be at the exact time you don't want to be there. And then takes away all means of escape so you have to fight through the situation as best you can.

Regardless of how thoroughly I plan, something always seems to go wrong.

I wouldn't have found myself in the mess with Ben Howard if I hadn't paid a short visit to my mother and my grandmother in Church Point, Louisiana. And I wouldn't have made that trip if I hadn't solved a big murder case in Stafford, Texas, just outside of Austin, a case that earned me a promotion, a five-thousand-dollar bonus, and a week's vacation.

Two days before my vacation was over, I headed back to Austin. I had no intention of visiting Ben, but on impulse I detoured off I-10 to Galveston, deciding to drop in on my old friend, a former Austin P.D. detective who now worked for the Galveston P.D. We could have a fast dinner, and I'd be back on the road.

Galveston was farther off I-10 than I figured, so by the time I reached the island city, I had decided to spend the night. I found a room at the Sea Gull Motel on Seawall Boulevard.

Ben and I had worked a few cases together over the last two or three years in Austin. He was a crusty, irascible curmudgeon, but he was fair, and he had an intuition that pedestrian P.I.'s like me salivated over.

He was wearing a harried look when I first spotted him in the squad room. When he saw me, he grinned. He seemed to be genuinely pleased to see me.

Later, we had a leisurely steak dinner at Gui Lee's. That's when he told me of the trouble that was set to blow Galveston Island into a prime candidate for gang war.

GUI LEE'S WAS crowded with laughing, carefree customers who savored the cuisine and appreciated the quality of the champagne. After my last bite, I patted my stomach. "I could hit the sack right now."

Ben chuckled and touched a match to his cigarette. He leaned back in his chair. "I can't remember the last time I got to bed before midnight since I got here."

"That busy, huh?"

He snorted and gulped a swallow of beer. "Be glad you're in Austin, Tony. This place is fixing to get busier than a call girl at a political convention."

When I frowned, he continued. "We're tiptoeing a fine line between a gang war and peace."

I leaned back and stared at him, thinking he was pulling my leg. "Gang war? Today?"

He took a deep drag from his cigarette. The smoke drifted lazily upward from his parted lips. "Throwbacks. Neanderthals. 1930s déjà vu. Sam Maranzano out of Chicago and 'Mustache Pete' Abbandando from L.A."

I whistled softly. I'd heard the names, but never figured they were in this part of the country. "Hard to believe."

Ben shrugged. "Yeah. Abbandando settled in here five, six years ago, so I've been told. Stevedoring operation. Perfectly legit, but an ideal front for a smuggling operation. Last year, Maranzano showed up in Houston."

"And that's when the trouble started?"

He shook his head and took another gulp of beer. "Not really. No trouble at all, but there's a tension in the air, like electricity searching for a ground. Something is going on, but I can't get a hand on it."

He grew silent, staring at his plate.

After a few strained moments, I cleared my throat. "Ready to leave, Ben?"

He looked up and blinked, as if seeing me for the first time. "Huh? Oh." He chuckled and shook his head. "Sorry. Yeah, let's get out of here. Let me show you our fair city."

WE PAUSED ON the sidewalk outside the restaurant. Ben looked up and down the Strand, then nodded in the direction of the Galveston docks. "Let's take a walk."

"Sure." I fell into step with him as we headed down the damp sidewalk toward the wharves. It was late, and the streets and sidewalks away from the Strand had little traffic. Ten minutes later, the gunfire broke out.

HALF A DOZEN uniforms were standing in two small groups in the ICU waiting room when I arrived the next morning. They eyed me malevolently. I forced a grin. "What's the word on Ben Howard?"

A pot-bellied sergeant stepped forward. His gray hair was thinning everywhere except on his eyebrows and the tops of his ears. His silver nametag read *Sgt. J. Wilson.* "In a coma."

I frowned, surprised. "Coma?"

A younger uniform elbowed his way through the wall of scowling lawmen. "You got a lucky break there, buddy."

Somewhere I lost the thread of conversation. "What do you mean?"

He grunted and grinned knowingly at his friends. "You know what I mean. As long as Howard's unconscious, he can't dispute your claim that you killed Frank Cheshire in self-defense."

His words rocked me back on my heels. For a moment, I thought I was hearing things. I looked from one face to the other. The expression on their faces left no doubt in my mind that they believed I wasted Frank Cheshire deliberately.

The next remark convinced me of that fact. "Yeah," added another cop. "As far as we know, you could have done Howard and Cheshire both."

A flush of anger burned my ears. I glared at the cop who had made the last remark. As usual, I spoke before I thought. "Before you run off at the mouth too much, buster, you better get your facts straight, or I'll poke them down your throat."

A rumble of murmurs greeted my threat. As one, they stepped forward. From the anger on their twisted faces, there was no question in my mind they were ready to put me in the ICU. I clenched my teeth and doubled

my fists, wondering how many I could kick in the groin
before they ripped my arms off and stuffed them down
my throat.

A young cop with fewer muscles in his head than on
his brawny arms stepped forward. "Let me have him,
Sarge."

Sergeant James Wilson said nothing, but from the
gleam in his eyes I knew he was considering the request.

A clipped voice behind me stayed them. "That's
enough, men. Get out of here. Get back on the job. You
too, Sergeant."

For a moment, they hesitated, a pack of dumb goril-
las with the collective IQ of a refrigerator bulb. The sergeant eyed me a few more seconds, then waddled away.
The others followed.

I turned and eyed the slender man in a three-piece
suit facing me. His chin was narrow, but his eyes were
steady. His short hair was parted on one side. To say he
was neat would be an understatement. Not a hair was
out of place, not a wrinkle in his suit. The knot of his
tie nestled exactly in the middle of his collar. His shirt
cuffs extended the socially accepted three-quarters of
an inch beyond the cuffs of his coat.

"Thanks, mister." I started to say more, but the hos-
tility burning in his eyes made me pause.

"You Tony Boudreaux?" He wasn't native to the coast
or Southeast Texas, for he pronounced the "X" in my
name instead of leaving it silent.

"Yeah. Boudreaux. No 'X.'"

He sneered. "Oh, now you're a smart guy, huh?"

I fought to control my temper, which was fraying badly. "Look, buddy. I don't know what you or your friends' problem is, but leave me out of it. I've known Ben Howard for several years, and I just came by to see how he was."

The sneer on his angular face deepened. "He's in a coma, that's how he is. And I'm not about to leave you out of our problem because you are our problem."

I stuck my face in his. "And who are you?"

A smug gleam of satisfaction filled his eyes. "George Briggs, District Attorney. I'm the guy who's going to strip you of your license and indict you for the murder of a cop." Before I could reply, he continued, "Of a cop you swore to kill."

His assertion stunned me. How did Briggs find out about a threat I made when I was young, ignorant, and unable to handle my booze? Then I realized I had an arrest record in Galveston, even though it had occurred more than fifteen years ago. The charges were dismissed, but the arrest record, like fallen arches, remained.

"You deny that?" He eyed me steadily.

I kept my eyes on his. I wasn't about to give him the satisfaction of looking away. "I don't deny it. But that was years ago. A bunch of us were at the beach. Spring break from college. I'd had too much to drink, and I just ran off at the mouth."

He arched an eyebrow. "Yeah. That's what you say

now. We'll let the grand jury decide, Boudreaux." He deliberately pronounced the "X," then leered at me.

"You got nothing to go on, Briggs. You're going to have to prove intent. My weapon was back in the motel. It was Howard's piece I used on Cheshire. Now you tell me how you're going to get intent out of that." I was growing angry again.

His thin lips spread into a smug grin. "You and Howard struggled for the gun. You got it and shot him, then used his piece on Cheshire when he tried to stop you. Simple."

I stared in disbelief. "You'll never make that stick."

"No? Just watch. I can do anything I set my mind on. You got my promise on that."

I remembered then what it was about Frank Cheshire that had set me off at the beach that day. His arrogant sneering. The Galvestonian mindset that cops were gods, and all the rest of us were peons for them to treat as they saw fit. Briggs was the same.

BACK AT THE MOTEL, I called my boss in Austin. Needless to say, Marty Blevins of Blevins Investigation was none too pleased to hear of the mess I'd managed to get myself in.

"Once Ben comes out of his coma, he can tell them what happened," I explained.

Marty snorted. "If he comes out. I've seen 'em lay there for years. And then croak. Jeez, Tony. You really fouled up this time."

I shook my head. Good old Marty. He had a knack for lifting a guy's spirits. "Listen, Marty. This D.A. down here has me worried. He came on awful strong. I can't leave town, but I can't just sit around and do nothing."

"No problem. I know a good lawyer down there. My cousin, Ernie—Ernest Blevins. Get in touch with him. He'll do what he can."

I REPLACED THE RECEIVER and plopped down on the bed. With a grimace, I realized I'd forgotten to call Janice Coffman-Morrison, my significant other and heiress to one of the largest fortunes in Texas, the Chalk Hills Distillery. We had made plans for tonight, but since I had no Starship Enterprise transporter chamber to beam me up, there was no way I was going to be in Austin by nine that night.

THREE

NEEDLESS TO SAY, Janice was disappointed, but she understood. We really had a perfect relationship. She understood when she wanted to understand, and I understood when she wanted me to understand. Simple and uncomplicated, like us. And neither of us wanted to complicate things with marriage.

She and I met a few years back when I helped her out of an insurance jam. Because of her money, she had no interest in a serious relationship and believe it or not, despite her money, neither did I. We had fun together even though I quickly realized I was simply a dependable escort, an occasional lover (at her whim), and a frequent confidant.

Ergo, a tool to satisfy her needs. And she was the same for me. We had reconciled our positions in our relationship. And we both were fairly content.

Inexplicably, despite the skewed relationship, we were very good friends who enjoyed each other's company. Personally, I'd never been able to figure out "our relationship," as Janice referred to it, but then, I really never worried about it. I seldom paid serious attention to those psychological or personal relationship things. I let the women worry about that sort of thing. I just said "yes" or "no" at what I considered the appropriate occasions. That usually kept me out of trouble and warded off any worries.

Now I was more worried about the D.A. His threats had me jumpy as a three-tailed cat at the local daycare center. Meeting Marty's lawyer cousin, Ernest Blevins, didn't help. In fact, after talking to good old boy Ernie for a few minutes, I began wondering just how many dots you had to connect to pass the Texas bar exam. By the time I left his office around mid-morning, I figured throwing myself on the mercy of the court might be my best option, next to slashing my wrists.

To sort out my thoughts, I took a walk when I left his office and ended up at the docks. The sun shone brightly out of a clear winter sky.

Despite the cutting wind howling out of the north across Galveston Bay, forklifts zipped across the docks, great shore cranes swung massive loads from cargo holds to waiting flatbeds, and conveyor belts whined and strained, transporting goods from the darkened caverns of great ships into cavelike warehouses. Stevedores scurried in every direction across the dock, over the ships, into the warehouse like ants on a wedge of chocolate cake.

I retraced our steps of the night before across the wharf. Stains, smeared now by footsteps and rubber tires, remained where Ben had fallen. I crossed to where Cheshire had gone down, then backtracked to the giant shore crane from around which he had emerged the night before.

Beyond the crane, a small section of the wharf had been cordoned off, the portion that had been poured the night before.

The freshly poured cement, a patch about twenty feet by twenty, appeared to be curing well. I noticed a footprint in the cement and grinned, remembering the times I wrote my name and left a footprint or handprint in every piece of fresh cement I ran across.

I made my way slowly along the orange ribbon, idly looking out over the newly constructed loading dock. The last patch of cement appeared to be the final piece of the construction.

I had no idea what I was looking for. I was just looking, hoping for an answer to fall from the sky and land at my feet.

One end of the orange ribbon was tied to an industrial Dumpster. The dock at the base of the Dumpster was littered with trash that had fallen from the front-end loaders when they dumped their loads.

There were broken TVs from Taiwan, crushed boxes of computer chips from Mongolia, stained and ripped clothing from Thailand. To add to the mix was a conglomeration of detritus such as shattered wooden pallets, broken furniture, a bent and twisted stove, a refrigerator with the door ripped off, and the toe of a wingtip shoe protruding from beneath a pile of seed corn spilled from a ripped bag.

At that moment, the piercing "beep-beep" of an approaching loader caught my attention. I waved and stepped from its path. Immediately, the driver dropped the bucket and scooped up the trash by the Dumpster, quickly depositing it just in time for a Kenilworth tractor to back up to the Dumpster, hook a two-inch cable to it, and winch it onto his rig.

"Some operation, huh?"

I jerked around at the voice behind me. "What?"

A freckle-faced redhead who appeared to be in his mid-thirties nodded to the disappearing Kenilworth. "The way these guys operate. They don't waste no time." The wind ruffled his hair.

I looked around as the Kenilworth disappeared around the corner of a warehouse. "It's a big operation here."

He shrugged down into his topcoat. "Yeah. I like to come down and eyeball them every so often."

For several moments, we watched the activity on the docks. Finally, he cleared his throat. "You the guy who shot the cop last night?"

For a moment, his words didn't register. When they did, I frowned at him, surprised. "What?"

Keeping his eyes on a cluster of stevedores unloading a truck, he replied, "The guy what shot the cop last night. That you?"

I grew wary. "Why?"

He shrugged. "If you are, Mister Abbandando would like to see you. My name's Augie."

Abbandando? I frowned, then I remembered what Ben Howard had said. Abbandando was the alleged crime boss who'd settled into Galveston several years earlier and set up what appeared to be a legitimate stevedoring operation.

What did he want with me? "Were you out here last night?"

Augie shook his head. "No."

"How did you know I was?"

He shrugged again. "Mister Abbandando knows. He told me to bring you to him."

I studied Augie several moments. So "Mustache Pete" Abbandando wanted to see me. I glanced over my shoulder, half expecting to see one of Galveston's finest observing our little conversation. To my way of thinking, such a meeting would be poor judgment on my part. Extra fodder for the D.A.'s pitch to the grand jury.

"What if I say no?"

An icy look flashed in Augie's eyes, quickly replaced with amusement. He grinned. "Then I suppose Mister Abbandando would have to come to you." He paused and hooked his thumb over his shoulder in the direction of the warehouses. "But, it would be more convenient for you since he's up in his office over there. Warmer, too."

"Over there" was a warehouse that stretched a quarter mile from end to end. Above the white metal building was a bright red sign reading MARITIME SHIPPERS. A panel of windows spanned the breadth of the fourth floor. A figure in a white suit stood in one of the windows. I couldn't tell which direction he was facing, but I had the feeling he was watching me.

I threw caution to the wind. I was in enough trouble now. Meeting "Mustache Pete" couldn't cause me any more. "Why not?"

"MUSTACHE PETE" ABBANDANDO was a tall, corpulent Italian in a white three-piece suit with which his large black eyes contrasted sharply. I saw instantly the source of his sobriquet, "Mustache." It was not a compliment. The mustache was thin, almost miniscule, out of place on the broad expanse of shiny flesh between his nose and upper lip.

Given his height and girth, a full-bodied, barbershop handlebar would have been much more appropriate.

No, the nickname was definitely not a compliment.

I wondered if he was smart enough to figure it out. Even if he weren't, I knew no one dared use the moniker in front of him.

But, to be honest, "Mustache Pete" Abbandando was a convivial host.

He crossed the expansive room and extended his hand. "Ah, Mister Boudreaux. Thank you for coming." He gestured to a bar at the end of the room. "I have coffee, cappuccino, or your choice of drinks."

I eyed the assortment of alcohol on the shelves behind the bar wistfully. Before I could give myself time to reconsider, I replied, "Coffee's fine."

He led me to a table in front of a wide expanse of

windows. The table was expensively appointed with a linen cloth, china glassware, and silver urns.

"Good view," I replied, sliding into the chair he indicated.

He waved a single finger, and a thin waiter with the sharp features and cold eyes of a hatchet man magically appeared.

"Word is, Tony—can I call you Tony?" he asked as he slid into the chair across the table from me.

"Sure."

"Good." He smiled broadly. "Call me Pete. Now, the word is, Tony, that last night after the last cement truck dumped its load, you shot and killed Frank Cheshire."

I studied him warily, hoping he wasn't measuring me for a cement jacket. "Was he important to you?" I sipped the coffee. Hot and rich, but without that extra wallop that Louisiana coffee packed.

He grew thoughtful, lowering his gaze to the coffee, which he was stirring slowly with a silver spoon. His heavy jowls sagged toward the cup, and his fat lips glistened in the reflection of the sun through the windows. His mustache reminded me of a single pencil line on a sheet of typing paper.

Keeping his eyes fixed on the coffee, he shook his head. "You have nothing to fear from me, Tony. The truth is, I'm looking for one of my own men. My cousin, Albert Vaster. He is the son of my mother's third brother. He is a good boy, but he is missing. I think he might have been, for reasons that are unimportant to you, following

Frank Cheshire. Since you were the last to see Cheshire alive, I thought perhaps you might have seen Albert. My men have searched the island for little Albert. He is nowhere to be found." He handed me a snapshot. "That was taken two months ago at his mother's birthday. He dances there with his mother."

I studied the picture. Little Albert Vaster was a handsome young man in his thirties, around six feet or so. I shook my head. "Sorry, Pete. I'm new in town. All I can tell you is about the restaurant last night and the docks later. If this man was there, I didn't see him."

Pete sipped his coffee, his eyebrows drooping like an injured pup. "Tell me about the shooting, if you don't mind."

"Sure. Not much to tell. Cheshire shot my friend four times, then tried me. I got him instead." I shrugged. "And that's all it was."

"Why would he do this?"

"Beats me." I shook my head. "We were just walking along and then there he was."

"You didn't see the one running away?"

"Nope."

"Mustache Pete" stared out the window. He pursed his lips. He drew a deep breath and looked around at me. Finally, he said. "Frank Cheshire was dirty, Tony. Dirty as a cop can get. I think—no, I truly believe—he killed my Albert. Maybe last night." He turned his eyes back to the window.

I leaned back in my chair, wondering why Pete had revealed his suspicions to me, a stranger.

He continued. "The truth is, Albert had the idea Cheshire was up to something, something that would affect us. I think that is why Albert was killed."

I respected the portly man's concern, but emotions colored by anger and hot-blooded family pride made for shaky, impulsive judgments. "Was Cheshire on your payroll?"

He turned back to me, his black eyes slits. After a moment, a slight sneer twisted his thick lips. He smoothed his tiny mustache delicately with his little finger. "At one time. Not for a year now. I think he was working for Sam Maranzano."

I don't know why I kept asking questions. Curious, I suppose. I should have known better. Being nosy always caused me problems. "Who's he?"

"A Sicilian thug. Sam Maranzano out of Chicago. He moved to Houston last year."

"Muscling in?"

"Mustache Pete" arched an eyebrow and looked at me slyly. "Not so you can see. He is sneaky. I think he is waiting for the right moment, which," he added with a touch of bravado, "I will not give him."

"If your cousin was following Cheshire last night, then he was on the wharf. Did your boys check the bay for him?"

He shrugged. "Sometimes two, three days before bodies come to the surface. Sometimes the currents carry them into the Gulf. Sometimes they are never found."

I looked out the windows at the broad bay stretching far to the north. Without warning, there was a sharp pop. Faster than the eye could discern, the window shattered into five gadzillion spider webs, then imploded back into the room.

I didn't know what had happened, but I wasn't crazy enough to hang around and find out. Even before the first chunk of shattered glass hit the floor, I was on my belly next to the wall. "Mustache Pete" was waiting there for me.

At that instant, the doors burst open and half a dozen button men packing an eclectic collection of Uzis, AK-47s, and even an ancient Thompson rushed to the window, throwing their bodies up as shields for "Mustache Pete" Abbandando.

Pete looked up from where he was huddling next to the wall, gave me a crooked grin, and grunted, "All in a day's work."

I had to admire his insouciant unconcern. I tried to appear as nonchalant. "I hope not. This is the only suit I own."

Pete chuckled. "I like you, Tony."

"Don't see no one, Boss," said a voice.

A second chimed in. "There's a boat in the bay heading for Texas City."

Pete grunted and pushed to his hands and knees. With help from two of his boys, he struggled to his feet, but

I noted he was careful to stay away from the windows. I brushed myself off and looked out the window from across the room.

Augie indicated a small hole in the ceiling near the far wall. "The boat, Boss. Had to be."

Pete nodded. "Do it."

I didn't know what the cryptic reply meant exactly, but I lay odds it boded nothing well for those in the boat.

Taking my elbow, Pete guided me to the bar in one corner of the room. "After that, I need something stronger than coffee, Tony."

I slid up on a stool. "Tempting, but I'll settle for water and a twist of lemon if you have it."

He arched an eyebrow.

With a sheepish grin, I explained, "Some of us can't handle the hard stuff."

Behind us, several workmen scurried in to put a temporary patch on the window.

To my surprise, Pete built both our drinks himself. While he did, I glanced at the snapshot partially crumpled in my hand. I smoothed it out on the bar. Yep, Albert Vaster was a nice-looking young man. I paid closer attention to the picture. He and his mother were dancing the tango.

The reason I knew it was a tango was that a few years earlier, I'd taken some dance lessons in an effort to prevent embarrassing Janice when we attended one of her country-club shindigs.

The only dances I knew when we met were the Cajun

two-step and the Church Point Stomp. In the joints I frequented, these steps were classics. But I discovered quickly that they were frowned upon at the Barton Springs Country Club when the club's executive director threatened to throw us out of the season's opening ball if we danced another step of either.

Seems like Austin society frowned on high kicks and Cajun howls.

I studied the snapshot, noticing the wingtip shoes Albert wore. I couldn't help remembering the single wingtip I'd spotted back by the Dumpster on the wharf earlier.

Unseeing, I lifted my gaze and stared at the handful of repairmen at the window. A couple of wild ideas flashed into my head.

"Mustache Pete" must have been puzzled by the thoughtful contemplation on my face. "What? You think of something?"

"This picture." I handed it to him. "Did Albert always wear shoes like that? Wingtips?"

The heavyset man squirmed around in his chair so that the overhead light shone on the picture. "Yes. He always wore wingtips. Said the wingtip was the shoe of a gentleman." He looked around at me. "Why?"

I held my hands up, palms out. "Now, there is probably nothing to this, but this morning before Augie came up to me, a front-end loader scooped up a bunch of trash and dumped it in a commercial Dumpster beside the new concrete they poured down there." I nodded to the window. "I saw a black wingtip on the dock."

Pete frowned, the wrinkles deep in his fleshy forehead. "I don't understand. We import thousands of shoes from Taiwan. You think it might be Albert's?"

"Like I said, there's probably nothing to it, but the shore crane where I spotted Cheshire last night is directly in front of the Dumpster. If Cheshire did waste your cousin, he could have tossed him in the Dumpster to be covered by trash before dumping at the landfill."

Pete studied me a few seconds, then his eyes grew wide. He grabbed the phone and barked a few orders into it, after which he replaced it and leaned back. "My boys will find the Dumpster. Thank you, Tony."

"Like I said, there might be nothing to it."

"Yes. But on the other hand, there might be."

I changed the subject. "You get many drive-bys like that?" I nodded to the window.

He shrugged. "Nature of the business."

"Rough business."

He smoothed his miniscule mustache. "Most are."

Thinking back over his last remark, I tended to agree with him. The toughest job I ever had was teaching English to kids who didn't want to learn in a high school that didn't want you to teach. The kids split their infinitives with knives and dangled participles out the third-story window. As far as the intellectually challenged administration was concerned, a syntactical relationship between a noun and adjective was the standard plot of a B movie.

I downed my coffee and slid off the barstool. "Wish I could tell you more, Pete, but that's all the help I can be."

He nodded. "For that, I thank you."

FOUR

BACK ON THE WHARF, I called the hospital on my cell phone. Ben was still in a coma, which meant I was still in limbo.

More than once, I'd seen a poor huckleberry get himself thrown into the slammer with no lawyer, no outside help, and end up on the short end of a hard-time verdict.

The D.A.'s threat the night before still bounced around in my skull. Indictment for murder meant I would lose my license. And just after I'd finally proven my old man wrong.

Before he abandoned Mom and me, he said I'd never amount to anything. Well, I did. I worked my way through high school, through college, and now I owed no one. No one except my boss, Marty Blevins. I'd made something of myself, and no one was going to take it from me. My old man, wherever he might be, wasn't going to laugh at me.

I drew a deep breath and stared unseeing at the squalling and diving seagulls overhead. I couldn't afford to wait for Ben to wake up. Like Marty said, he might not, and if he didn't, I was in alligators up to my neck.

At a brisk pace, I headed back to my pickup. I had

work to do in my motel room. And the work began with Frank Cheshire. I wanted to know as much about him as I could.

I UNLOADED MY LAPTOP and booted it up. My desktop came up with a picture of Oscar, my albino tiger barb. He was the single exotic fish remaining in my aquarium after my old friend Jack Edney murdered the other fish by urinating into the aquarium.

Unfortunately, Oscar didn't survive intact. He suffered brain damage; now he only swam in tiny circles.

Like most murderers, the next morning Jack had demonstrated remorse, blaming his act on his drunken state at the time.

My landlady tended to Oscar while I was gone, so I knew he would be well fed.

I quickly reconfigured some of the Internet options and dialed my local service in Austin. I called up the website of Eddie Dyson, computer whiz, entrepreneur, stool pigeon, and reformed thief. Eddie had built himself a lucrative business selling information online.

He had upgraded the questionable occupation of stoolie into that of online executive and capitalist, taking payment only by credit card. Other than his innovative system of delivery, all the old guidelines still held true. No questions asked and keep your mouth shut.

The truth was, I never wanted to know where he found his information. I ordered a full report on Frank Cheshire.

Shutting down the computer, I pulled some notecards

from my briefcase and started with a few random questions. Why did Cheshire try to kill us? What was he doing on the wharf? Why was Albert Vaster following Cheshire? What kind of job was Cheshire doing for Maranzano?

And my most important question: am I starting in the right place?

I knew "Mustache Pete" wouldn't give me any information about why Albert was tailing Cheshire. So that was eliminated. I could wait for Eddie's reply, or I could contact the Houston or Galveston newspaper, or I could seize the moment and march into the Galveston Police Department. Maybe I could find some help there.

Before leaving for the police department, I called the hospital. No change with Ben.

AT THE POLICE STATION, I hoped the duty sergeant would call Sergeant Wilson to the front desk, but instead he sent me back to the squadroom. I grimaced, crossing my fingers that the uniforms I had run into at the hospital earlier were either off or out on beat.

Hesitating at the door to the squadroom, I looked around, spotting two or three familiar faces. Then I saw Sergeant Wilson. He looked up from the papers on his desk and stared hard at me. I marched across the room, ignoring the whispers.

I stopped at his desk. "Sergeant."

His light blue eyes made me think of ice cubes. "What do you want?"

"Ben Howard is still in a coma."

"So? What does that have to do with you? I asked what you wanted."

"Talk. I want to talk."

"Yeah? What about?"

I glanced around the squadroom. Every set of eyes was on us. I was getting in deeper and deeper. "Frank Cheshire."

He eyed me narrowly, then cut his eyes down at the papers on his desk. "I got nothing to say."

"Look, Sergeant. Regardless of what you think, I shot in self-defense. I just need the answers to a few questions, that's all. I want to find out just what was going on out there last night."

He snorted. "You know what was going on out there last night."

"If I did, I wouldn't be here."

"You ain't getting no help from me," he replied, keeping his eyes fixed on the paperwork before him.

I slammed the palm of my hand in the middle of his paperwork. "Why not? I'd like to know why."

Half a dozen uniforms rushed toward me as Wilson jumped to his feet and glared at me. "Because you murdered Frank Cheshire and maybe Ben Howard. There ain't no way I'm going to help no one who kills one of us. No way. You can rot in perdition for all I care." He waved the uniforms back. "Hold it, boys. Don't give this jerk-off no reason to claim police brutality."

My ears burned. I had a belly full of Sergeant Wilson. "So that's how Galveston boys operate, huh? Let's find a poor slob to pin it on and then throw the book at him. You ever hear of the Gestapo, Sergeant?"

Excited murmurs broke out. I kept my eyes on Sergeant Wilson. For a moment, indecision flickered in his eyes and quickly exploded into a blaze. He held up his hand. He drew a deep breath and studied me for a moment. Keeping his eyes on me, he said. "Sit back down, boys. I'll take care of this." He paused. "Call it what you want, but no one here is going to talk to you about Frank Cheshire. No one. So, Mister Boudreaux, if you're smart, you'll get out of here and not come back."

Deliberately, I looked around the room, fixing my eyes on each uniform staring at me. Then I turned back to Sergeant Wilson. "Sergeant, I'll be back when I want, and you'd better not be hiding anything from me."

I don't know why I made that last threat. It just seemed the thing to do.

I HEADED BACK to the motel, wondering why I ever thought I might get some help from Galveston P.D.

The phone was ringing in my room when I opened the door. I picked it up. "Yeah. This is Boudreaux."

A guarded voice mumbled, "Cheshire was fooling around with some kind of smuggling deal for Sam Maranzano."

I couldn't believe my ears. "Who is this?"

"You don't need to know."

"Okay. I don't need to know. Now, what about…"

"No more. The Blue Wall is too strong to fight."

A dial tone sounded before I could ask my next question. I replaced the receiver. The Blue Wall. Cop togetherness. One for all, and all for one.

Truth was, I couldn't blame them. They had a dirty, thankless job, constantly walking a tightrope of life and death. And at the most unexpected moment, a twist of fate could topple them in one direction or the other.

Still, I couldn't help wondering who made the call. One fact was certain, however. The anonymous caller was not Sergeant Wilson.

Maybe I'd been wrong about the Galveston P.D. At least there was one who hated dirty cops. Unless—unless I was being set up to take another fall.

At least Abbandando's allegation that Cheshire worked for Maranzano had some support. Maybe I needed to pay another visit to "Mustache Pete" Abbandando.

AUGIE OF THE red hair and freckled complexion and another of Pete's button men, who bore a striking resemblance to Godzilla, stopped me as I reached the elevator for Pete's private office. "I need to see him," I said.

Pursing his freckled lips, Augie studied me, then nodded to Godzilla. "I'll see."

He picked up the wall phone and spoke into it. I couldn't tell what was going on. He'd nod, then shake his head, then nod.

I cleared my throat. "Tell him I know about the smuggling."

It was a wild stab, but it hit the mark. Stunned disbelief flickered across Augie's face for a brief instant be-

fore a frown erased it. "Ah…hey, yeah, Boss. He says…"
He cupped his hand over the mouthpiece and whispered.
He tried to keep his eyes on the telephone, but they kept
cutting nervously back to me. He nodded. "Yeah. Okay.
Okay, Boss."

So far, so good, I told myself as I took the elevator
up to the fourth floor. The smuggling angle must have
some substance. Augie reacted, and obviously Pete had,
or else I wouldn't be going up to see him.

PETE'S EARLIER CONVIVIALITY had gone south. He didn't
even offer me a chair. He sat. I stood. Two of his men
stepped between me and the elevator at my back.
"Smuggling is against the law," Pete said and then remained silent.

"Yeah. Last I heard, it was." I remained quiet. Two
could play this game.

After several moments, he cleared his throat. "Why
are you here, Tony?"

I glanced around at his boys. If he wanted me dead,
I was dead, so I shrugged and replied. "Here's the situation, Pete. I'm accused of murdering Frank Cheshire
and shooting Ben Howard. Now, if Ben pulls through,
I'm off the hook, but—"

Pete finished my sentence for me. "He croaks, you
croak."

With a chuckle, I said, "I might not have put it as col-
orfully, but that's it. If I can figure out why Cheshire
was out there, maybe that will tell me why he shot at

us. He had to believe we were someone else. The fog was so thick, you couldn't make out who someone was until you were right up in their face. You said Albert was following him."

He arched an eyebrow and nodded briefly.

"All I had this afternoon was a number of disconnected incidents. Then I got an anonymous call less than an hour ago. The caller said Frank Cheshire was involved in a smuggling deal with Sam Maranzano."

I paused, then added, "Now, maybe I'm wrong, Pete, but when I add one and one, I come up with two. When I add my anonymous call, you telling me Cheshire and Maranzano worked together, Albert following Cheshire, Albert disappearing, Cheshire shooting blindly at two figures in the fog, I could come up with someone trying to hide a smuggling operation. Now, if Cheshire is trying to cover up something, and Albert is following him on your orders, then any way you slice the bread, you're involved with the caper."

A foot shuffled behind me, but Pete shook his head almost imperceptibly and the shuffling ceased. Keeping his fat hand curled in his lap, he straightened a thick finger in my direction. "You think I smuggle?"

I shook my head. "I don't care about the smuggling. I got my neck to look after. I've worked too long and too hard to have everything blow up in my face because of someone like Frank Cheshire. I'm going to prove he was dirty, that he was involved with Sam Maranzano,

and that he shot at us because he believed we were following him."

He dragged his tongue over his fat lips as he studied me. Finally he said, "What do you want from me?"

"Why was Albert following Cheshire?"

"Mustache Pete" drew a deep breath. "Our sources
gave us information that Maranzano had hired Cheshire
to pick up a lead on one of our South American opera-
tions." He paused and reached for a cigarette from the
open case on the table at his side.

South American? That could spell dope.

"Why would he cross an operation like yours? He'd
have to know he was playing with dynamite." Then I remembered Ben Howard alluding to a possible gang war.

With a shrug of his rounded shoulders, Pete grunted.
"Who knows the mind of another. I say to Albert, 'Albert, you follow Cheshire. Do not contact him. See
where he goes.' That is all I said to Albert. We know
nothing of this smuggling."

The story rang false.

Why should Maranzano and Cheshire risk trouble by
stealing drugs from an established operator when there
were enough fly-by-nights out there for him to put together his own shipment of anything from Wild Cat to
Magic Smoke?

I had the distinct feeling Pete was putting out a false
trail. Why? Obviously, the shipment was even more
valuable than a truckload of Johnny Go Fast and Lady

Snow. I didn't figure to learn anymore from Pete, but I gave it a shot.

"Who could he have been working with? Maybe some friends?"

Pete lit his cigarette. "Frank had no friends." He arched an eyebrow. "But, we hear Maranzano, like you."

"Was the shipment coming in by water?"

Pete made a sweeping gesture with his hand. "Up and down the coast, there are many bays and inlets. Every night, goods are brought in. If I brought in goods, that is how I would do it. But I stay legal, Tony. That time of my life is behind me."

I resisted a grin. I'd have to win the Texas lottery before I'd believe "Mustache Pete" Abbandando had put that life behind him. I took a step back. "Well, thanks anyway, Pete."

A look of sad remorse settled over his pan-shaped face. "I wish I could tell you more."

"Me, too. Me, too."

My reflection stared back at me from the polished steel wall of the elevator. I grinned at myself. Pete didn't fool me. He was mixed up in some smuggling deal that Maranzano was trying to horn in on. That was the only explanation for Albert tailing Cheshire—to see just how much Cheshire knew of the caper.

Whatever it was, I'd wager a thousand to one it wasn't drugs.

I had to have solid evidentiary proof linking Cheshire to the smuggling caper before the police would believe me. That meant I had to find someone who knew that Cheshire was involved in the deal, the goods being smuggled, and when they were due. Three fragments that to me made up a whole.

It didn't take a research scientist to know that without the last two fragments of information, the Galveston P.D. would never believe the word of the first.

As I climbed in my pickup, I spotted "Mustache Pete" looking down from his fourth-floor office. My skin crawled.

A WISE MAN once made the remark, "Shallow men believe in luck." Well, shallow or not, I believed in it. And for once, it smiled on me, because when I got back to the motel room, Eddie Dyson had discovered the answer to two of the questions I had just raised.

Unfortunately, he gave me more than I bargained for.

FIVE

Diamonds?

A thousand bucks?

I don't know which stunned me the most, the goods being smuggled in or the charge Eddie hit me with for digging up the information.

Excited, I reread his message for the tenth time. I had my contact and the goods. Two pieces of evidence. One to go.

According to Eddie, Cheshire used an intermediary to approach a fence named Ho Lui in Philadelphia concerning uncut diamonds. Only once, three weeks earlier.

"Diamonds," I muttered, staring out the motel window at the surf beating against the seawall along the shoreline of Galveston Island. So much for Abbandando and South America. I figured he was blowing smoke. But why?

On the other hand, diamonds made sense.

A fortune in diamonds, even after fencing, could fit into a coffee can, a size easy to smuggle and hard to discover. Especially in the hold of a cargo vessel your own stevedores are off-loading.

At the end of the message, Eddie enclosed a copy of his bill for the information: a cool grand. I knew he was a genius with the computer, but what kind of hoops did he have to jump through that cost a grand?

I read the message again, this time looking for the identity of the intermediary, the contact I needed to support my allegation that Cheshire was dirty. There was no name.

I frowned, puzzled that Eddie had forgotten to provide me the identity of the go-between. He was usually extremely thorough.

For a thousand bucks, I wanted the name. I had to have the name. Whoever he was, he was the key I needed to prove Cheshire was dirty. I reached for the motel phone, then hesitated. It was probably bugged. I grabbed my cell phone and headed for the parking lot, where I punched in Eddie's number.

He picked up on the first ring. His initial affability cooled as soon as he recognized my voice, not too perceptibly, but enough for me to pick up on it.

"You all right, Eddie?"

"Sure, sure, Tony. You get the stuff you ordered?" It came out "yougetthestuffyouordered?" He rushed his words together, giving me the feeling he wasn't too anxious to talk to me.

I shook my head. Just my imagination. "Yeah. You must have run into some problems, from the charge you laid on me."

He chuckled nervously. "Sophisticated technology today, Tony. Satellites and all that stuff. There ain't nothing secret anymore." He seemed to be relaxing somewhat. "You think it was too steep?"

The afternoon traffic began to build on the thoroughfare paralleling the seawall. I turned my back and cupped my hand over the mouthpiece.

"No. Good information. That's what we pay for. Hey, the guy who approached the old boy up north. You didn't give me a name. That's why I called."

There was a strained pause.

"You hear me, Eddie?"

"Yeah. Yeah, Tony. I hear."

I sensed the reluctance in his voice. "What is it, Eddie? What's going on?"

"Well, I…you see, Tony, I…ah…"

Something was wrong. Eddie was as glib and garrulous as a sideshow huckster, unabashedly pushing his wares and beating his chest. He wasn't the kind to stammer and stutter.

I grew impatient. "What are you trying to tell me, Eddie? Spit it out."

Behind me, a car honked. I jumped and looked around.

An older woman with a disgusted look on her face stared at me from behind the windshield of a new Mercedes. Here we were in the middle of an empty parking lot a hundred feet wide, and I'm in her way? I stepped aside, and with a sharp sweep of my arm, waved her by. She squealed past, thanking me with an obscene gesture.

Eyeing the Mercedes malevolently, I continued my

conversation with my stoolie. I was growing more impatient. "Come on, Eddie. What's wrong?"

"You ain't going to like it, Tony."

I shouted, "Let me decide! Now who is it?"

"Okay, okay. Take it easy. It's a guy in the Morrison family. He's your girlfriend's cousin."

"Janice's cousin? But she doesn't have…" Then, with a groan, I remembered. Theodore Morrison, the long-lost cousin from the black sheep side of the family. He had popped up a few months earlier.

Eddie's voice was apologetic. "Sorry, Tony. I hated to spring it on you. It's a bummer."

I nodded slowly. "You're sure? Positive?"

"Hey, for the kind of jack I charged you, I'd sign in blood. This Morrison guy met with the gentleman in Philadelphia. The old boy's got no reason to lie about it."

"Is the fence going to deal with Morrison and Cheshire?"

"Too risky. He wouldn't say why, but I got the feeling some big guns were involved."

"What about an address for Morrison?"

"Can't find one. This Morrison bird stays outta sight."

"See if you can find one. He's supposed to be working for some law firm. At least, that's what he told Janice and her aunt. Maybe it's in Galveston or Houston."

For a moment, Eddie didn't reply. Finally, he said, "I'll give it a shot."

I should have been tickled to have another lead, and

such an important one. Maybe I would have been, had the news not made me sick to my stomach.

Back in my motel room, I added to my initial notes. There is one unequivocal, indisputable, incontestable fact. Evidence does not lie. It cannot be intimidated. It does not forget. It doesn't get excited. It simply sits and waits to be detected, evaluated, and explained.

Witnesses may lie, lawyers may lie, judges may lie, but not evidence. And since it doesn't, then enough must be gathered to make a logical interpretation.

That was what I was attempting to do: gather enough evidence and hope I interpreted it correctly before Ben Howard died.

Other than my significant other's cousin being involved, I felt better about the case I was building against Cheshire. I had no idea about the extent of Ted Morrison's role in the caper, but he was the proof I needed that Cheshire was mixed up with the smuggling. I had to find him.

Morrison wasn't listed in the Galveston or Houston directory, nor in the white pages on the Internet. I hadn't expected to find him, so I wasn't disappointed.

I called my boss, Marty Blevins, in Austin and put him onto Morrison. "Get me anything you can find, Marty. Address especially."

"Theodore Morrison? He kin to the old lady that owns Chalk Hills Distillery."

"Long-lost cousin."

Marty snorted. "Jeez, bet that ticked off that little gal of yours when he showed up. Wasn't she the only heir?"

I could hear Marty chortling. He got his jollies from other people's back luck. "Yeah."

"Where'd this guy come from?"

I knew all the details, but I didn't figure it was any of his business. Just give him something else to jeer at. "Beats me. Just see what you can find."

"You bet, kid. Ben still in the coma?"

"Yeah."

"Well, you know what they say. Let's all hang in there together, or they'll hang us all." He laughed so hard at his joke that he started choking. Ben Franklin probably rolled over in his grave when he heard his famous remark butchered so.

I hung up. For several moments, I stared at the silent receiver in my hand. Ted's sudden appearance a few months earlier had rocked the entire Morrison family. Beatrice Morrison, matriarch of the clan of two, had more money than the Bank of England, and she spent a bundle checking Ted Morrison's claims. All the paperwork was in order. Even DNA.

Theodore Morrison was a third cousin to her dead husband. Best I understood, Theodore was the third generation from a brother of her deceased husband's father. Something like that. I usually had trouble understanding relationships beyond mom and dad.

Being reared an orphan with no family other than her Aunt Beatrice, Janice had enthusiastically welcomed

Ted into the family. The fact he would be entitled to an equal amount of her inheritance was not an issue. How could it be, when the two of them would share several hundred million?

But I could imagine her reaction when Janice heard the accusations against him. I could imagine what she would say to me when she learned I was the one who brought them.

THREE SHARP KNOCKS on my door jerked me back to the present. I frowned. "Who…" My words trailed off as I rose and headed for the door. The hair on the back of my neck bristled.

Hesitating, I glanced about the darkening room, for some reason taking comfort I had not turned the lights on.

The knocking sounded again, this time more urgent.

Without touching the heavy drape covering the front window, I peered through a tiny crack between the thick material and the wall. A brawny man in an expensive suit and wearing a five o'clock shadow on his square jaw stood at the door. He was one of those guys so muscular, he looked out of place in a suit, regardless of how expensive.

I couldn't see his right hand, but in my imagination, it was in his coat pocket, folded around a .44 Magnum. He knocked again with his left.

I had a bad feeling. I had no idea who he was, but I wasn't about to open the door.

He twisted the knob and grimaced. Then he retrieved a plastic card from his coat pocket and dropped it in the lock slot. I grew tense, ready to make a dash for the door if it opened.

He twisted the knob again. The door remained locked.

Abruptly, he turned on his heel, slipped the card in his pocket, and strode hastily down the gallery. Moments later, a sweat suit-clad couple passed in front of my window.

I studied the parking lot, but my visitor had vanished. He could have been anyone. As far as I knew, maybe he was here to announce that I'd won ten million dollars, but to be on the safe side, I strapped my .38 to my belt.

Pushing my visitor from my mind, which was like trying to ignore a 600-pound gorilla banging at the door, I ran back through the snatches of information I had picked up earlier in the day. Cheshire was trying to smuggle diamonds into the country and Morrison was looking for a fence. If Cheshire was working for Maranzano, then in all probability, so was Morrison. I wasn't sure where Abbandando came in, but he was part of it.

Chances were, Cheshire fired at Ben and me thinking we were some of Abbandando's button men who had stumbled onto his caper.

But what was he doing out on the wharf at midnight? With the fog so thick, no ships were coming in. Even the cement truck crept through the fog. I hesitated, frowning. I suddenly had the eerie feeling I knew more about that night than I thought I did.

Now, I know there are some romantic souls who enjoy strolling in the fog. I had strong doubts, however, that Frank Cheshire was one of them. Whatever reason he had for being on the wharf had to be important, so important and so secretive that he started shooting before he even knew who was out there.

I knew I couldn't count on help from Galveston P.D. any more than I could from Sam Maranzano. The only move I had left was to break into Frank Cheshire's apartment. See what I could find.

As soon as I located him, I'd track down Morrison.

And then I'd worry about Janice's reaction.

SIX

CHESHIRE'S NAME WAS in the telephone directory. "That was simple," I muttered, jotting down the address and slipping it into my shirt pocket. "Now, if getting into his place is half as easy..."

Throwing on my windbreaker, I opened my door and looked up and down the second floor gallery for the gorilla who had been banging at my door. He was nowhere around, so I headed for the stairs. I rounded the corner and froze, one hand braced against the soft drink machine at the top of the stairs.

My earlier visitor was halfway up the stairway. We stared at each other in surprise for a couple of seconds, and then I did the first thing that came into my mind.

I shoved the soft drink machine down the stairs at him.

He yelped and jumped back. I followed the clattering machine as it bounced and scraped down the stairway like the proverbial runaway train.

Showing surprising agility for someone his size, my visitor hit the base of the stairs one step ahead of the soft drink machine and leaped aside, slamming into the brick wall across the walkway. His head bounced off the wall. With a groan, he sank to the concrete.

I was two steps back. Before he could move, I whipped out my .38, grabbed him by his lapels, and jerked him upright, at the same time sticking the silver muzzle of my revolver into his left nostril.

His eyes grew wide. "Don't shoot, don't shoot," he whispered.

I jerked his lapel. "Who are you? What are you doing here?"

He gulped hard, then stammered, "I…I'm your body-guard."

All I could do was stare at him blankly. I pulled him into the light. "You're what?"

He gulped again. "Yeah. Ernie sent me. I'm your bodyguard."

"I don't know any Ernie." I shook my head, expecting a trick.

"Blevins. Ernest Blevins. Your lawyer."

At that moment, a figure appeared behind him at the corner of the walkway. He shouted, "Hey! What's going on here? What are you guys doing to my machine?"

"Your machine?" I shouted back, at the same time slipping the .38 back into my pocket. "You the manager here?"

"What's going on?" He was growing belligerent. "You're tearing up my place."

I always had a knack for lying. Usually I managed to keep it under control, but this time I turned it loose on him. "You tell me. My friend here and I were heading up the stairs here when a couple of kids shoved the drink machine down on us. We could've been hurt bad. You're lucky we don't sue you anyway."

His belligerence vanished. He rushed forward. "You guys hurt anywhere?"

I brushed at my bodyguard's suit. "I'm fine. How about you, George?"

My bodyguard blinked a few times. "Huh?"

"I said, 'Are you all right, George?'"

"Oh, yeah." He flexed his arms. "Yeah. I'm okay." Then he winced and jerked his foot off the concrete.

The manager gasped. "What? What? Something busted?"

Placing his foot gingerly back on the ground, the heavily muscled man put some weight on it. He grimaced, then gave a faint smile. "No. I think it's okay."

The manager breathed a sigh of relief. "That's good."

I fixed him with a hard stare. "You better find those boys. This was deliberately malicious. We're just lucky one of us didn't get hurt bad."

He nodded emphatically. "Yeah. Yeah. Don't worry, Mister…ah…"

"Boudreaux. Tony Boudreaux. I'm in 256."

"Mister Boudreaux. Don't worry. I'll find them."

"Come on, George. Let's go on up to my room and take care of business."

George limped after me.

I CLOSED AND LOCKED the door behind my bodyguard, then turned on the light. I kept my hand in my pocket, clutching the .38. "Okay, start at the beginning. What's this all about?"

He shook his head. "My name ain't George. It's Virgil."

I nodded. From his size and bulk, he didn't look like a Virgil. Maybe a Derrick or Rocky, but not a Virgil. "Okay, so it's Virgil. What's this all about?"

He looked around the room uncomfortably. "Alls I know is that Ernie…I mean, Ernest Blevins, hired me and told me to stick by your side so nothing would happen to you." He shrugged. "That's it."

I raised a skeptical eyebrow. "You didn't do much of a job out there on the stairs."

He shrugged and gave me a sheepish grin. "I'm not really a full-time bodyguard. I'm a bodybuilder. Last month I competed in the IFBB's Mr. Olympia contest. Third place," he added with a broad grin.

A bodybuilder! That I could believe, but a bodyguard? "How'd you get into this bodyguard stuff?"

With the guileless innocence of a child, he explained. "Oh, Ernie lets me do it between competitions. I pick up some cash before I start training for the next competition. Besides, Ernie says it helps his tax return." He shrugged. "I don't understand how, but that's what he says."

I rolled my eyes. Great. Now I had a part-time bodyguard, part-time bodybuilder at my side. Still, I liked him immediately. I don't think he could have told a lie if he wanted to, but I had to be sure. I dialed Ernie.

IN A SNAKE-OIL smooth voice, Ernest Blevins said, "I don't know all the details, Tony. All I know is that "Mustache Pete" Abbandando sent word to put a shield on you. When I asked him why, he said that someone had shot out one of his windows."

"Yeah. I was there. So what?"

"So," Ernest replied. "That slug wasn't meant for Pete. It was meant for you."

I remained silent, stunned by the news.

"Tony? You still there?"

"Huh? Yeah. Yeah, I'm here. How did Pete know that? I mean, how did he know the bullet was meant for me?"

"He didn't say, but he has ways of finding out that sort of thing. Now, listen, Virgil is strong as an ox. He can run his head through a door. He's got muscle. All you have to do is point him in the right direction. Cousin Marty says you're a bright guy. You got the brains, Virgil's got the brawn."

I thought about how easily I had taken Virgil out at the stairway. "Well, hey, thanks, Ernie. That makes me feel real good. You hear anything from the D.A. today?"

"Naw. Takes them old boys a while. Even if Briggs pushes the case against you, it'll take him two or three weeks before he can take it to the grand jury. By then, Ben Howard will be awake."

"You hope."

"He will be. Trust me."

Trust me! That's probably what Delilah said to Samson when she gave him the knockout drops. "Yeah.

Right." I replaced the receiver. Sorry, Ernie, I told myself. I don't trust anyone except my mother's son. I gave Virgil a crooked grin. "Ernie speaks highly of you."

Virgil grinned shyly. "Thanks." He plopped into a chair and removed his shoe so he could massage his injured foot. "He's my cousin."

With a rueful grin, I shook my head. Now, why hadn't I guessed that? My boss, Marty, sends me to his lawyer cousin, Ernie, who in turn gives me his muscle-bound cousin for a bodyguard. A classic example of good old American nepotism, with all the attendant tax breaks.

With a sigh of resignation, I plopped on the bed, trying to figure out why someone would take a shot at me. A rank odor curled under my nose. I ignored it, concentrating on who might have tried to waste me—if they indeed had. I needed to talk to Pete about both the alleged attempt on my life and my significant other's cousin, Ted Morrison. But first, I wanted to get into Cheshire's place before anyone else. With Virgil, at least I'd have someone to keep an eye out.

The rank, horsy odor grew stronger. Was there a dead rat in the walls? I wrinkled my nose. Sitting up, I saw Virgil massaging his bare foot. That was no dead rat.

He looked up as I headed for the door. "Let's go, Virgil. We got some business to tend." I opened the door so fresh air could blow inside.

In the pickup, I glanced at Virgil. "You know where 23rd Street is?"

He nodded.

"The Tradewinds. An apartment complex."

He gave me a sappy grin. "My cousin owns the place."

I looked at him in disbelief. "Another cousin?"

"We're a big family." He grinned.

A big smile popped out on my face. I'd been trying to figure out how we could get into Cheshire's room, and now all my worries were over.

I waited in the lobby while Virgil went into the office. Moments later, he returned with the key. "Any problems?"

He shook his head. "No trouble, but the police just left. Plainclothes guys."

"Police?"

"That's what Willard said." When I frowned, he explained. "Willard. My cousin."

CHESHIRE'S APARTMENT WAS middle-of-the-line rental property, about five or six hundred a month. A snack bar separated the living area from a small kitchen. A bedroom opened off one wall. The bath opened into the bedroom. In general, the apartment was fairly neat, something of a surprise since Cheshire was a confirmed bachelor.

Standing in the open doorway and surveying the apartment, I said, "Your cousin said the police were here?"

"Yeah. Why?"

"No reason." I shrugged and stepped inside. Against one wall sat a yellow vinyl couch with a claw-footed coffee table in front. Two occasional chairs that didn't match were on either side of the coffee table. Against another wall was a cheap desk with a computer.

I didn't doubt someone had searched the room, but I would have given staggering odds it wasn't the police. I have yet to see a search scene that didn't look like a bomb had exploded when the police completed their search. Cheshire's place looked like he'd just stepped out for a pizza.

Which led me to another puzzling conclusion. If the cops hadn't searched the place, then who? Abbandando? Maranzano? Or Morrison?

The reason was obvious even if the identity of the previous searcher wasn't. Cheshire had information about the smuggled diamonds and someone wanted that information.

I locked the door behind us, then hesitated. Other than Eddie Dyson's report, I had no substance, no solid foundation for any of my theories. All I was doing was guessing.

"What do you want me to do?"

Virgil's question jerked me back to the present. "You start in the kitchen. Look for anything—notes, pictures, anything. If it's got writing on it, I want to see it."

He looked at me like I was simple. "Okay. If that's what you want."

I started in the living room, searching for telephone numbers, names, dates, any information I could find. Later I would winnow through the chaff and keep the wheat.

Whoever had been in here earlier must have heard

about the impressions left on telephone pads, for the pad was slick as the gumbo mud back home. Still, I gave it a shot, but the pencil marks revealed nothing.

I searched the desk for bills or scribblings, but found none. I booted up the computer and went to the history file. It was clean. I nodded in appreciation at someone's thoroughness. "But, let's see just how thorough," I muttered, going five or six steps deep into the operating system.

Bingo! Someone hadn't gone far enough back to clean up the files. Back in the temporary Internet files there were hundreds of addresses.

Quickly scrolling through those for the last six months, I jotted down all the transportation addresses. The fact they were all maritime struck me immediately. I also recorded addresses for several stevedoring firms and two buoy manufacturers.

Then I searched the bedroom.

Seagulls didn't pick fish bones any cleaner than the bedroom. Several suits, slacks, and sport coats hung on the rack. A pair of running shoes, two pairs loafers, and one lone shoe hung upside down on shoe trees.

I picked up one of the loafers, a brown Brioni with a leather tassel. Size eleven and a half with a ribbed sole. I stared at the shoe, remembering the footprint I had spotted in the fresh cement back at the wharf. If I wasn't mistaken, the print was the same as the sole of the Brioni.

I checked the other shoes. All Brioni. Well, Cheshire had taste in shoes, at least.

"Find something?"

Virgil's question jerked me around. I kept everything close to the vest. "Nope. Not here. What about you?"

"Nothing."

I wandered back into the kitchen.

A telephone directory lay on the snack bar. Several numbers were scribbled on the cover. I copied them. Probably pizza or hamburger delivery joints. One had the word "Allied" beside it.

I glanced under the cabinets. The usual bug sprays, over-flowing trash beginning to ripen, a few cans of paint—one with ribbons of red paint dried on the side, another unopened, and a collection of dollar store pots and pans. Nothing out of the ordinary.

As an afterthought, I flipped to Maritime Shipping in the yellow pages. I wasn't sure what I was hoping to find, perhaps a circle drawn around a shipping line with a note stating, "This is the one" or perhaps a shipping line corresponding with one I found on Cheshire's computer. No such luck.

Except for the Internet files and the phone numbers, the place was clean as a freshly scrubbed floor.

OUTSIDE, STARS SPARKLED in a black sky. We stopped off at a hamburger joint along the seawall and picked up a bag of double-deckers with fries. During the ride back to the motel, I planned the next couple of steps. I wasn't crazy about Virgil tagging after me the rest of the evening, listening to what I said, learning what I learned.

I didn't trust him—not completely, not yet. Whatever I found, I wanted to keep it to myself.

After we ate, I'd get rid of Virgil. Then I could follow up on the websites, call the numbers we found, visit Pete, and check the shoe print in the fresh concrete at the wharf.

At the thought of the fresh concrete, a tiny idea formed in the back of my head, so nebulous I couldn't put my finger on it, but it was there, nagging at me. I remembered the unsettling feeling I had earlier that I knew more about that night than I thought.

VIRGIL DIDN'T ARGUE when I told him I was going to hit the sack early. He nodded and left. I watched from the window as he descended the stairs and crossed the parking lot to the front of the motel.

He seemed like a nice guy. I felt a twinge of guilt, but I didn't know him well enough to trust him. As far as I knew, he might be the kind to hit the nearest bar and blabber his head off.

No, what I had to do tonight, I could best do alone.

SEVEN

LEAVING MY .38 BEHIND, I grabbed my coat and jumped in my pickup. I didn't know if "Mustache Pete" was still at his office or not. If I missed him, at least I could assure myself that the footprint in the cement had the same configuration as the Brioni in Cheshire's apartment.

I checked the flashlight in my glove compartment.

From time to time during the short drive to the docks, I glanced in my rearview mirror, wondering if the police were still tagging after me. I didn't spot anything unusual.

AUGIE STOPPED ME at the warehouse door. By now the fog had settled in. He grinned. "Not a good night to be out, friend. This stuff will be too thick to drive in."

"I'll make it. Pete around?"

He shook his head. "Left an hour ago."

"My lawyer called me. Said Pete told him the slug that shattered the window today was meant for me."

The expression on Augie's face didn't change. He shrugged deeper into his coat as a chilling blast of air swirled around us. He glanced past me, then opened the door wider to the dark warehouse. "Come on in out of the cold."

"Thanks."

"Over here," he said, indicating a lonely circle of light under a glowing radiant heater mounted to a steel ceiling joist. He stopped beneath the heater. "This is better."

I nodded, savoring the sudden heat dispelling the chill. "Yeah."

He studied me a moment, his hands still jammed in the pockets of his topcoat and the collar turned up about his neck despite the warm air blowing over us. "I like you, Boudreaux. I don't want to see nothing happen to you. Pete don't either."

"How'd Pete know those bozos were shooting at me?"

A crooked grin curled his lips. "Our boys met the boat across the bay. By the time they finished with those two, the shooter was spilling everything he knew."

"Who paid them?"

Augie shook his head. "Contract. Five G's in an envelope with your John Hancock inside."

I blew out through my lips. "Short and to the point, huh?"

"Business is business."

"Any guess who might have paid them?"

"Wasn't Pete." Augie pursed his lips. "Might've been Sam Maranzano, but there's no proof. If that smuggling business you was talking about is on the level, maybe one of those players. Hard to say."

At least I had the answer to one question: how Pete

knew the slug was meant for me. That didn't help with Cheshire or Morrison.

BACK IN THE pickup, I stared at the warehouse. I was gathering quite an eclectic collection of facts. I grimaced in frustration. When were they going to start making sense? Or were they? Maybe like my old beagle, Bat, I was waiting at the wrong hole for the rabbit. He never once caught a rabbit, but he was always waiting at a hole.

With a soft curse, I started my truck and eased cautiously across the dock to the freshly poured concrete next to the Dumpster. Visibility was zero. Suddenly, the orange ribbon cordoning off the fresh cement leaped out at me. I slammed on the brakes. Climbing out, I left the lights on dim.

I knelt by the footprint. The headlight beams shattered on the tiny beads of moisture filling the air, blurring details of the imprint, but when I ran my finger over the impression, I felt the ribbed imprint of Cheshire's shoe. Well, well, well, what do you know, I thought. Maybe this rabbit is in the hole.

Footsteps sounded behind me.

Instinctively, I ducked, and a sharp blow struck the back of my shoulder. I hit the wet concrete and rolled through the standing water to my right, out of the glare of the headlights into the darkness. The footsteps hurried toward me. Still on my back, I kicked out with my feet and slammed into someone's knees.

There was a grunt and a curse. A body bounced off

the fender of my truck. I rolled to my feet just in time to see my assailant lift his arm once again. I did what any all-American boy would do. I kicked him where it hurt most.

He froze in midswing. A groan of agony hissed through his lips just before I slammed a knotted fist into the blur that was his face. I felt something give, and when he staggered backward, a dark film covered his chin. I hoped I'd busted his nose.

In the next instant, he spun and, still holding himself, waddled to the edge of the wharf and leaped into the darkness.

Breathing hard, I stood on the dock watching the white foam his leap had created fade away. I heard him swimming somewhere in the darkness below. A dull throb pounded in my shoulder. Clenching my teeth, I rubbed it. At least nothing was broken.

I didn't have time to gloat about my good luck, for another voice broke the silence of the night. "You took care of him, buddy. Let's see what you do with us."

Spinning, I saw two hulking blurs less than six feet from me. Their hands were in the shadows of their bodies, but I had the feeling that they weren't just clutching fog.

"Yeah," said a second, guttural voice. "It's time for you to take a long, long swim underwater."

I made a promise to myself right then. If I ever made it back to Austin, first thing I would do is enroll in one of those karate or tae kwon do courses that teaches a guy how to beat up on a dozen bad guys at the same time.

Suddenly, a shadow appeared from the darkness around the Dumpster. It was nebulous, but whoever or whatever it was, it held something over its head.

With a shout, the shadow leaped forward and swung.

One of the goons facing me screamed and dropped to his knees. The second spun as the shadow swung again. The second thug squealed like a pig and grabbed his arm. The shadow swung again, driving both thugs toward the bay.

Not wanting to impede my benefactor's progress, I scurried aside several feet, peering into the fog at the indistinct figures and rubbing my sore shoulder.

Moments later, there was one startled scream after another followed by two splashes of water.

The shadow remained motionless, then turned toward me. A thousand crazy thoughts raced through my mind. What if this guy was some kind of psycho who thought he owned the docks? What if he came after me? I held my breath.

That didn't help. He started toward me.

I took a step sideways, ready to jump in the bay.

A voice broke the silence. "Tony! You okay? Hey, Tony!"

"Virgil? That you?" I stared at the vague silhouette in disbelief.

He drew closer, and I made out the baseball bat in

his hand. "Yeah. You shouldn't of left without me, Tony. There's bad people here who want to hurt you."

I glanced at the darkness beyond the wharf. "Yeah," was all I could say.

"You sure you're okay?"

"Well, I'll have a sore shoulder, but, yeah, Virgil, I'm just fine."

"Then why don't we go back to the motel?"

"That's the best suggestion I've heard all night. By the way," I said as I reached for the pickup door, "How'd you find me?"

"Oh, I just stuck a bumper beeper on your pickup. I'm supposed to take care of you, don't you remember?" he replied simply, walking past me and disappearing into the fog. His disembodied voice echoed from the gray mist. "Go ahead. I'll get my car and follow."

A bug? I gaped after him. He bugged my truck. I grinned. Not bad, for a bodybuilder. Not bad at all.

The grin on my face vanished as I pulled out of the dock gates. Apparently, "Mustache Pete" failed to make believers out of those who had taken a potshot at me. Otherwise, where had the three goons who jumped me on the wharf come from?

THAT NIGHT, I DREAMED of baseball bats, oversized goons, and icy water.

I was glad when morning came.

Sipping on a cup of hot coffee, I visited the websites I had discovered on Cheshire's computer. I wasn't quite sure just what I expected to find, but whatever it was, I didn't find it.

If diamond smuggling was the reason Cheshire had been at the docks, then I could make a case against half a dozen shipping lines as being the carriers of the goods. Each of the lines made contact of some kind with South Africa, a blanket assumption I made as to the source of the diamonds.

By mid-morning, I had finished downloading the available information from each website. Later, I could sit at the snack bar in my motel and go back over the data with a greater degree of detachment.

Then I started on the telephone numbers I'd copied from Cheshire's telephone book. The first number was an adult movie house, the second, Joe's Pizza, and the third, the local newspaper. Remembering the cement truck from two nights before, I arched an eyebrow at the fourth number, the Allied Cement company. There was no answer at the fifth number, 555-3636.

As I replaced the receiver, the phone rang.

A guarded voice whispered. "The D.A. stashed some coke on the back of the vanity drawer in your room."

Before I could say thanks, kiss my foot, or take a hike, he hung up. I couldn't tell if it was the first caller or not.

I yanked the drawer out. There it was, a nice clear plastic bag taped to the back of the drawer. I ripped it off, then yanked open the other drawers. Just the one.

Hurriedly I ripped it open and dumped it, shredded

bag and all, in the commode and flushed it all down the drain.

I was paranoid by then. Frantically, I searched every hiding spot in the motel room. They were all clean.

And just in time, for there was a sharp rapping at the door followed by a belligerent voice. "Boudreaux. This is the police. Open up."

I folded the list of websites and telephone numbers into my pocket and calmly opened the door.

Four uniforms leered at me. An unfamiliar sergeant stuck a folded piece of paper in my hands. "Search warrant, Boudreaux. Step back."

Taking the warrant, I did as he said. "By all means, Sergeant. You gentlemen come right in and help yourselves. I'll just sit over here out of the way and watch TV."

They didn't even put on a good show of searching. After glancing around the room for five seconds or so, the sergeant pulled out the vanity door. "Just as I thought. Cok…" The word died on his lips. He frowned, turned the drawer upside down, then tossed it on the bed and pulled out the other drawers.

All clean.

They promptly tore my room apart, but found nothing.

I clucked my tongue. "Gee, Sarge. Looks like someone gave you boys a bum tip."

He glared at me, a crimson blush spreading up his neck and covering his cheeks. "Yeah?"

I shrugged. "Seems that way. Sorry you went to all the trouble for nothing."

He stammered, finally managing to mutter a curse as he stomped out of my room. I couldn't resist the opportunity. "You old boys come back now, you hear? And, by the way, tell Sergeant Wilson I said hi."

EIGHT

A FEW MORE CURSES drifted up from the parking lot, but the squeal of tires on the macadam was a truer measure of the policemen's frustration. I stood in the open doorway, staring at the cruisers disappearing into the traffic. I struggled to make some sense out of what was going on around me.

"You all right, Tony?" Virgil stood in the open doorway of the room next to mine. He closed his door behind him.

"I had some guests."

He grunted. "Saw 'em. Figured it was best for you if I stayed out of sight. The less they know, the better off we are."

"Come on in," I said, turning back into the room. "I could use a drink if I hadn't taken the pledge."

Inside, I poured us some coffee as I told him about the warning call, not so much for information he might provide as to bounce my theories off him. "I don't know that the D.A. set me up. All I have is the caller's word, but this is the second time he's been right."

"The second?"

"Yeah. First time, he said Cheshire was mixed up in diamond smuggling. Another source verified that."

He shrugged his shoulders, his white shirt fitting over his heavily muscled torso like spandex. His sleeves were rolled up to his elbow, revealing forearms as thick as my biceps. "You must be on to something, huh?"

"Why would the D.A. try to frame me? What did I do that would make him go south?"

"Maybe he wants to make certain the grand jury indicts you."

I studied Virgil a moment. His answer made as much sense as any I could come up with. "Maybe so. Anyway, sitting around here is getting us nothing." I slid my cup back on the snack bar. "Grab your coat, Virge. We're going to pay Allied Cement a visit."

ALLIED CEMENT WAS on the mainland, north of Galveston on the outskirts of Texas City. A few battered signs along Highway 146 into Texas City touted a *Beautify Texas City* project from the previous decade.

A privacy fence of weathered cedar surrounded the ten-acre site in an obvious effort to follow the city beautification guidelines. Perched on a maze of steel beams in the middle of the yard, four giant cylindrical silos towered over fifty-foot high cone-shaped piles of gravel and various aggregates. Like pieces of a Rube Goldberg creation, half a dozen whirring conveyor belts carrying large buckets filled with sand and gravel ran in a dizzying mélange of angles from the ten-foot square hoppers on the ground to the top lips of the silos.

The whine and roar of straining diesel engines filled

the air as front-end loaders dumped aggregates and sand into the hoppers in an unending procession. Bright yellow cement trucks sat rumbling beneath the silos, waiting their turn for the next load of ready-mix concrete.

A blast of cold air greeted us as we climbed from my truck. I tugged my jacket around me and hurried for the dispatch office.

Inside, a welcome flow of warm air rolled over us. A grizzled clerk of about fifty and wearing a Houston Astros cap nodded. "Howdy, boys. What can I do for you?"

In the glassed-in office behind him, a younger man with a round face glanced up and frowned.

I pulled out my wallet and flashed my identification, the private security card issued by the state. I explained, "There was a cement truck a couple nights back around ten o'clock on the docks near Maritime Shippers. Can you check your job register or log to see if it was one of yours?"

The old guy frowned. "Do what?"

"You keep a record of trips the trucks make?"

His frown deepened. He nodded. "Yeah. Yeah, so?"

"So, can you tell me if one of your cement trucks was on berth 21 in Galveston two nights ago at around ten o'clock?"

He saw the light. "Oh. Oh, yeah. Yeah, I can tell you." He reached under the counter and pulled out a thick book with a worn brown cover. He hesitated. "Now, who are you?"

Patiently, I pulled my wallet back out and opened it to my license.

At that moment, the younger man from the office came out, his forehead wrinkled in puzzlement. A roll of flesh hung over his belt. "Can I help you?" He gave the older man a glance that said: *I'll take over.*

"I hope so," I replied with an amiable grin on my face. I offered him my hand and introduced Virgil and myself.

He nodded. "Jerry Cook, Mister Boudreaux. I own this company."

I glanced out the window at his plant. "Nice operation you have here."

"Yeah. We're one of the first slurry mixers in this part of the state. You know anything about ready-mix?"

"Only that it gets hard."

He hitched his belt up over his ample belly. "Well, our process is more complicated than the competition's, but we turn out a better mix with a more thorough hydration and in less time than they do." He pointed to a vertical cylinder the size of a boxcar, the top of which was a terminus for several conveyors of sand and aggregate. "By the time the mixture passes through those giant blades inside that mixer, every cubic inch has been mixed and remixed."

A process about which I couldn't care less. I nodded politely. "Impressive."

He gave me a lopsided grin. "Like I said, complicated. But, you're not here to learn the concrete business. Right?"

I kept smiling. "As I told this gentleman, Mister Cook, I'm trying to learn the identity of the cement truck that delivered a load of cement to berth 21 in Galveston two nights ago." I hastened to add. "There's no problem. I just need to ask a couple questions, that's all."

The lopsided grin froze on his lips. He eyed me warily. "Are you the police?"

"No." I opened my wallet again. "Private investigator. And like I said, there's no problem for the company. All I need to find out is who contracted the job."

Jerry Cook shook his head. His voice had cooled perceptibly. "Can't help you, Mister Boudreaux. Sorry. It wasn't us."

From the corner of my eyes, I spotted the older man quickly cut his eyes furtively at Jerry Cook. "Are you sure?" I persisted. "Two nights ago?"

"Positive."

I glanced at the book. "You know without looking?"

"Yep. Foggy that night. We don't deliver in the fog. Causes problems when the concrete sets. Isn't that right, Pitt?"

The older man jumped, then nodded. "Huh? Oh, yeah. Yeah, that's right, Mister Cook. Don't set up good."

Cook was lying. I felt it in my bones, but I kept grinning like the proverbial possum. "Well, thanks anyway, Mister Cook. Appreciate the help."

"Anytime."

I stopped at the door and turned back. "By the way, you know a cop by the name of Frank Cheshire?"

The frozen smile on his face cracked, but he quickly covered it. "Nope. Never heard the name. That surprises me though, if he's from around Texas City. I know most of the force by their first name."

"He isn't from around here. Just thought you might have heard of him, but thanks again."

OUTSIDE, HIS SHOULDER turned into the cold wind, Virgil muttered, "He's lying."

"Yeah. That's what I guessed." I slammed the truck door. "And the only reason someone lies is because they're covering up something."

Virgil grunted. "Yeah."

I started the pickup. My stomach growled, reminding me that I hadn't eaten since the night before.

Virgil chuckled. "Somebody's hungry."

"Yeah. How about it?" I pulled into the traffic.

"You like chicken fried steak and fried potatoes?"

"With gravy?" I stopped at a signal light and glanced at him.

"And homemade rolls."

The light changed, and I moved with the traffic. "Just point us at it."

Mae's Home Cooking was on a side street a few blocks from the Strand. The small, unimposing frame building was packed, but the service was fast, and within thirty minutes we'd each put away a plate-sized chicken fried steak smothered with cream gravy, a heaping pile of crispy French fries, and half a dozen yeasty, butter-soaked homemade rolls.

"NAP TIME NOW." Virgil grunted when we climbed back in the truck. "Let it settle."

I laughed. "I won't argue that." But a nap was the last thing I had on my mind. I had a lot of work to do, and no idea how much time I had to do it.

Just as I closed the motel door behind me, the phone rang. "Yeah?" I wondered if it were my informant from the station.

"Boudreaux?"

The voice was different. "Yeah?"

"This is Jim Wilson, Sergeant Jim Wilson."

Instantly, I grew wary. "What can I do for you, Ser-geant?"

"I'm down in your parking lot. Off duty. I'd like to talk. Private."

My initial impulse was to refuse. If the D.A. were trying to set me up, what kind of tricks would the ser-geant try? On the other hand, he might be my pigeon at the station. I crossed to the window. "Where are you?"

"Red Pontiac. Facing you across the parking lot."

I spotted a face peering up through the windshield. "All right. Be right down."

Before I left, I informed Virgil. "Just watch in case he tries something."

"Don't do it, Tony. I don't trust any of the bluebirds."

"Just watch."

"Don't worry."

WILSON WAS NURSING a beer despite the open-container law the state had recently passed. He studied me as I slid into the shotgun seat.

"Sergeant."

He nodded. "Thanks for coming down. Ben's still in a coma."

"I know. I called earlier."

A tense silence followed, during which he seemed to be struggling with himself. I glanced around the parking lot, halfway expecting an army of uniforms to converge on me.

He chuckled. "Don't worry. It's just the two of us."

The tension lessened. "Okay. I'll take your word for it. Now, what did you want with me?"

He studied me another few moments, then cleared his throat. "I been a cop twenty-four years. This is a good department here, honest boys—most of them. You always have one or two rotten apples. I'm telling you that because I've been doing some checking on you. What I learned doesn't fit in with you trying to off Ben Howard. That confused me until I stumbled onto…well…" He hesitated. "Well, there's some at the station who aren't willing for the process to take its own course."

"You mean about the indictment and the grand jury?"

"Yeah. Some are going out of their way to build the case against you. I don't approve of that, but I can't bring myself to rat on my brothers. All I can do is offer my help, but on the Q.T." He eyed me steadily. "Understand. I'll deny everything if words gets out."

I took a wild stab. "You the informant?"

Wilson frowned and leaned back against the car door. He eyed me warily. "What informant?"

On impulse, I didn't mention the call claiming Cheshire was on Sam Maranzano's payroll. An honest cop resents one of his own being accused of being on the take. I didn't want to risk alienating Wilson. "I had a call from someone at the station. He tipped me to a surprise search of my room. Claimed the D.A. stashed some coke on me." I continued. "The caller was right. There was a bag of Lady Snow taped to the back of my dresser drawer. The cops went straight to it, but I'd already flushed it down the toilet."

His eyes widened in surprise. He whistled softly.

"Are you that informant?"

He shook his head. "No." He thought a moment. "I got no idea who it might be. Most of the boys hate your guts. I don't know who could have called you, but I'm not the one." He hesitated, then added, "I wouldn't take the chance on calling."

At least he was honest—or seemed like it. "You think my informant was right about the D.A. being behind the coke?"

Wilson chewed on his bottom lip. "I can't answer that."

"Can't or won't?"

He hesitated a moment, then grinned uncomfortably. "Won't."

That was good enough for me. "You mean what you said about helping on the Q.T.?"

He sipped his beer. "Yeah."

"I need an address. Morrison. Theodore Morrison. Ted for short. He supposedly worked with Cheshire on a recent deal."

"What kind of deal?"

I wasn't absolutely convinced of Sergeant Wilson's sincerity. I decided to play my cards close to the vest. "I'm not sure."

He grinned. "Okay. I got you. Give me some time. I'll see what I can find out."

"How do I get in touch with you?"

"Don't. I'll get in touch with you."

NINE

LYING ON MY BED with my fingers laced behind my head, I took another look at what I had, at where I stood, and at where I had to go. Except for a couple of nebulous ideas bouncing around in that empty container I called a skull, I wasn't much closer to having any answers than I had been five minutes after I shot Cheshire.

Oh, I had a lot of theories. The most compelling, though far-fetched, was that Abbandando set up the smuggling deal, and somehow Maranzano learned of it. Though Cheshire reportedly was on Maranzano's payroll, I waffled on whether the mob boss put Cheshire to work on the caper or Cheshire stumbled across it himself.

Regardless of who planned what, since Cheshire had Morrison contact the fence, it was obvious Cheshire was planning on diverting the shipment from whomever it belonged to, Abbandando or Maranzano.

He planned to hijack the goods himself and put the blame on Maranzano. Let the two big boys fight it out while he skipped out with a load of diamonds.

While I couldn't come up with any sort of connection between Cheshire and Allied Cement, I felt certain it was an Allied truck I had spotted out at berth 21 in front of Abbandando's warehouse. On top of that, it was Cheshire who had stepped in the fresh cement at the wharf.

And what about my informant at the station? Who could he be? Then there was Sergeant Jim Wilson. Was he on the level? Or was he part of the D.A.'s elaborate plan to stack the case against me?

But what really puzzled me was the true motivation behind District Attorney George Briggs's crusade to bury me for a lifetime behind the walls of Huntsville Prison.

I remembered one spring when I was a youngster. Grandpa and I were hunting deer along the spongy banks of a black-water bayou when a feral sow burst out of a thicket with the sincerest of intentions to slice us into sides of bacon and then stomp us into small patches of grease.

Grandpa put a 30-30 slug between her eyes, and she skidded to a halt in the spongy peat less than a yard from our feet. At that moment, squeals burst out in the briars and a dozen dark little shapes scattered in every direction, quickly vanishing into the thickets around us.

Grandpa slipped his knife from his belt and sliced the sow's throat. Bright red blood spurted out. "Son," he said, wiping the blade on his pants. "Whenever an animal comes at you for no reason, they're either crazy or protecting something."

And that's the only explanation I had for the District

Attorney's actions: he was either crazy or protecting something. And there was no way I figured he was crazy.

So what could he be protecting?

He already had enough evidence to get me indicted on the Cheshire shooting. So why continue building the case?

I rose and stared unseeing out the window at the gray waves rolling in from the Gulf. I had stumbled across more than I knew.

The jangling of the telephone snapped me from my reverie. It was Sergeant Wilson. "Got an address," he said.

"Shoot."

"Apartment 315, Seaview Plaza."

"What city?"

"Here."

Whoa. I didn't expect that. "Telephone number, by any chance?"

"Yeah. 555-3636."

I jotted down the number. It looked familiar, and then an alarm went off in my head. I stammered out my thanks and hung up.

Muttering an excited curse, I fumbled with the list of numbers I had copied from the cover of Cheshire's telephone book. There it was, the fifth number—the one that never answered.

I stared at the number on the notepad. Morrison might be able to deny making contact with the fence, Ho Lui, in Philadelphia, but what excuse could he have for his number being on the front cover of Cheshire's telephone book?

I reached for my jacket, then froze. Janice. What was she going to think? All those years with her Aunt Beatrice as her only kin, and then along comes Cousin Ted. Taking a deep breath, I shook my head and slipped into my jacket.

TED MORRISON LOOKED like he had stepped right out of a catalog, with short blond hair, tanned complexion, and a dazzling smile.

He covered his surprise at my sudden appearance and made an effort to be convivial, but beneath the surface he was as tense and defensive as a cur mongrel guarding a bone. I had the feeling he knew exactly why I was paying him a visit.

But he was the perfect host. We sat across from each other at the counter in his apartment. He sipped a cold bourbon and coke. I sipped ice water and eyed his bourbon. Don't let anyone fool you into believing booze is easy to leave alone.

Anyway, we made idle chitchat about our first meeting at the coming-out party his aunt had thrown at the country club in Austin a few months earlier.

He relaxed somewhat. After a few more minutes of inane chatter, during which we both grew restless, I jumped feet first into the purpose of my visit.

Briefly, I told him about the events on the wharf a few nights earlier.

He looked at me in surprise. "I...I read about the shooting, but I didn't have any idea that you were involved."

"Unfortunately, I was there—par for the course, as far as I'm concerned. Always at the wrong place at the wrong time. That's why I need your help."

"Me?" He arched an eyebrow. "How can I help you?"

"I know you had some business dealings with Frank Cheshire. I was hoping you might know what he was doing at the wharf so late at night."

Morrison chewed on his lip in concentration, but I sensed that he was making a show for me. "I never really had much to do with Cheshire. I really have no idea what he was out there for."

I couldn't blame him for being close-mouthed. He was playing a dangerous game with Sam Maranzano and Pete Abbandando, but he was also hammering nails in my coffin. I placed my elbows on the counter and leaned forward. I spoke softly, almost casually. "Look, Ted. I...no, we know you worked with Cheshire and that you contacted a fence by the name of Ho Lui in Philadelphia about some diamonds. Your telephone number was found on Cheshire's quick call list, and your number is listed more than once on the records from the phone company."

The last two assertions were blatant lies, but they worked.

A crimson flush rose beneath the smooth tan on Morrison's face. He sputtered over his reply. "How...but, I..."

I tossed in the fence's address to nail down the validity of my assertions. "Ho Lui's office in Philadelphia is on the corner of Market and 46th Street, in the Nineteeth Police District." I paused, staring at him.

He stared at me like a cornered animal, his eyes darting about frantically, searching for a way out. "No. No, you're wrong about that. You're way off base." He chewed on his bottom lip, this time out of nervousness.

It was at that very moment that I knew he was not a Morrison. Janice and I knew each other intimately, and I knew his Aunt Beatrice well.

While I sometimes sneered at their money and social posturing, I had always admired their cool aplomb in the middle of crises. Plop either of them on the stool across from me and they would have greeted this same accusation with a steel backbone and a look of defiance in their eyes so cold as to bring about a new ice age.

I shrugged. "Then if I'm off base, you won't mind if I turn this information over to Abbandando and Maranzano."

His face paled. He swallowed hard. His hand trembled as he fumbled in his shirt pocket for a cigarette. "I...ah, I wish you wouldn't," he mumbled. "I...I think there's some kind of misunderstanding here."

"Tell me about Cheshire, then."

Hands shaking, he touched a match to his cigarette. His face sagged in resignation. "Not much to tell. I ran into him at Sandy's."

"Sandy's?"

"Yeah." He gestured over his shoulder with the cigarette. "A bar down on Post Office Street. Cheshire gave me five big ones and a round-trip ticket to ask that Ho Lui guy about some diamonds. He wasn't interested. That's it."

His story stunk worse than Virgil's feet, but I went along with him.

"And that's the only time you had anything to do with him?"

"Just that once."

"How did you come to meet at Sandy's? I mean, did you go to him or did he look you up? Who contacted who?"

I could see the wheels spinning in his head as he fabricated his story. He frowned, a little too dramatically. "As I remember, I mentioned to the bartender I was running short on money. I asked him to keep an eye out for something."

I played along with him. "You don't work with the law firm anymore?"

The question surprised him. "Law firm? Oh, yeah, yeah, the law firm." Morrison was a terrible liar. He had no idea what I was talking about.

I grinned and gave him a break. "You remember. The one you were at when you discovered your cousin and your aunt."

His face lit in understanding. "Oh, yeah. The law firm. No. I don't work for them any longer. I did some investigative work for them, but the contract ran out.

I'm sort of between jobs, you might say." A smug grin curled his lips.

"You and Cheshire must have done a lot of talking about the deal. He had your name on the cover of the phone book, and the telephone records show eight or ten calls to your number."

The smile faded from his lips. "Well, maybe we did talk more. Yeah, now that you mention it, we did have several conversations about the diamonds."

"Did he tell you who he was hijacking the diamonds from?"

"Oh, no." He shook his head emphatically. "There wasn't no hijacking. The way he talked, a shipment was coming in. I assumed he brokered it. Strictly legit. He needed a buyer." A sly look slid over his face. "You know, I was wondering about that guy in Philadelphia. That's when I figured something was crooked. When I got back, I told Cheshire I didn't want nothing to do with nothing against the law."

"He must have given you some time, a date to pass on the fence in Philadelphia."

Morrison frowned.

I explained. "A timeline. Like when could he have the merchandise in Philly."

"Oh. No. Nothing like that."

He was lying again. What part of his story should I believe? None? Or all? Might as well flip a coin.

"But he did tell you about the diamonds?"

Morrison nodded briefly. "Yeah."

I vacillated a moment between asking him the question or keeping quiet. I went with the question. "Would you be willing to tell the police about the diamonds?"

His eyes grew wide. "Police? But why? What good would that do?"

"I need proof that Cheshire was dirty. He was smuggling diamonds."

Hastily, Morrison backtracked. "I didn't say nothing about smuggling. Like I said, it was legit."

I leaned forward. "But you also said you told Cheshire you didn't want to do anything against the law. Now which is it, Morrison? Make up your mind."

He frowned, trying to go back and remember just exactly what he had said. "I didn't mean against the law," he stammered. "That wasn't what I meant."

"Then what did you mean?"

He stared at me helplessly. "I don't know," he whispered. "But not that. I thought it was all legit. That's what I meant."

I glared at him. I should have known he would crawfish. And even if I subpoenaed him, he'd crawfish. I glanced at my watch. 10:30 p.m.

I climbed in my pickup where Virgil was waiting. I circled the block and parked across the street, banking on Ted Morrison to scoot to whomever was paying him.

While I waited, I bounced my ideas off Virgil. "After all is said and done," I added in conclusion. "I'm convinced he was working with Cheshire to fence the smuggled diamonds, but there isn't enough evidence to even justify a search warrant. And besides, Galveston P.D. wouldn't consider anything I requested."

"You think him and Cheshire was working for Maranzano?"

"Could be. When I mentioned Maranzano and Abbandando's name, he sure got nervous."

"What do you make of that?"

"I think it means we've got to keep an eye on both of them."

Virgil grunted.

To my surprise and disappointment, Ted Morrison didn't leave his room.

At two a.m., we headed back to the motel. The only pleasant thing about an otherwise disappointing and boring evening was that Virgil kept his shoes on.

TEN

I COULDN'T SLEEP.

Like a catchy tune that sticks in your head, a dozen
unanswered questions about Allied Cement kept tumbling over and over in my brain.

I was convinced it was an Allied truck I had spotted at berth 21, and I was convinced the footprint in
the fresh cement belonged to Cheshire. Fresh cement,
a wingtip shoe, a missing man. I shivered. Was this
what had been nagging at me about that night? Was it
possible?

On impulse I rose, dressed, and silently slipped
out. As I gently closed the door behind me so as not to
awaken Virgil, a raspy voice broke the silence. "Going
somewhere?"

I jerked around to see Virgil standing in his doorway.
I shook my head. "Not without you, it appears."

He nodded. "Where are we going?"

"I hate for people to lie to me."

"Morrison?"

"No. Cook. The guy at Allied."

With a chuckle, Virgil grunted, "Let's go."

A LOW-HANGING FOG had crept in from across the bay, hovering four or five feet off the ground. Oncoming trucks were only a blur above their headlights.

We pulled off the main highway and parked near the back corner of the Allied yard, which was partially lit by a few security lights sprinkled about the grounds. In the distance, foghorns bellowed out their eerie tones, hollow echoes that seemed to reverberate in every globule of the thick mist above our heads.

In a typically human example of foolish inconsistency, the locked gates in the gray privacy fence were within a dozen feet of a gap in the fence large enough to drive a truck through.

No dogs, at least.

We hurried through the fog to the office. With Virgil as lookout, I quickly picked the lock and we slipped inside.

The office smelled of stale cigarette smoke and mildew. The counter was directly in front of us, a solid black wall four feet high. Beyond, lit dimly by the glare of the security lights, was Cook's office. "Keep an eye out," I whispered, making my way to the counter. I leaned over and felt in the shelves. My fingers touched the logbook. "Here it is," I muttered, opening it on the counter and focusing my penlight on it.

I could hear Virgil breathing heavily at my side. I ran my finger down the dispatcher's list of jobs. I didn't really expect to find any substantiating evidence to support my half-baked theory, but to my surprise, there was a record of a job two nights earlier at berth 21, Galveston. I gasped. "Well, I'll be—would you look at this?"

Virgil muttered. "I knew he was lying."

Suddenly, the telephone rang in Cook's office. We both jumped, then froze. The jangling of the phone sounded like the clanging of cymbals. Finally, it stopped. Moments later, a tiny red light flashed on Cook's desk. Caller ID? "Wait here."

I slipped into Cook's office and crouched by the desk. The diffused glow of the security lights lit the interior of the office. I punched the new-call button and jotted down the number. On impulse, I punched the button again.

A grin the size of Galveston Bay jumped to my lips when I spotted a familiar number. 555-3636. Ted Morrison. 10:33 P.M. Three minutes after I had left his apartment. I punched the button again, but there was no more history.

I don't know where the mutt had been, but before I had a chance to gloat, a deep snarl sounded from the darkness in the back of the office. Instantly, I leaped for the door to the outer office, but the growling dog beat me to it. Through the window separating Cook's office from the outer office, I spotted Virgil heading out the front door.

That left the back door for me. The snarling animal's claws scrabbling for a hold on the slick floor gave me an extra shot of adrenaline as I jumped for the glass door.

The light from outside illuminated a fire extinguisher hanging on the wall beside the door. I ripped it from its hanger, tore off the safety tab, and hit the charging dog squarely in the eyes with a large dose of potassium bicarbonate.

He yowled and ducked his head, scrubbing at his eyes. I hit him with another charge and yanked open the glass door, slamming it shut behind me.

I didn't have time to catch my breath.

The door shattered.

At first, I thought the dog had leaped through it, but the splintering wood in the door jamb inches from my head told me someone was out there in the fog shooting at me.

I dashed for the shadows beyond the glow of the security lights. Another slug tore up the ground at my feet. I zigzagged, praying I didn't zig when I needed to zag. I headed for the piles of gravel and sand, hoping to lose my pursuers.

In my serpentine dash for the safety of the gravel piles, I'd forgotten about the dog. I didn't know what kind it was, but any dog coming for me is enough to keep me running. Then I heard him bark somewhere behind me.

I couldn't outrun him, but maybe I could outclimb him. I darted around a mountain of gravel just as a slug tore past me. I raced behind another pile and started climbing, sinking almost to my knees in the loose aggregate. Moments later, I heard a confusing mixture of growls, curses, and then two thumps, the unmistakable reports from a silencer. The dog yelped, then fell silent. The dumb mutt had chased the wrong man.

"Son-of-a..." I clenched my teeth and threw myself prone on the gravel, hoping to hide in the shadows cast by the security lights. Where was Virgil?

The only sounds were from the occasional vehicles sweeping past on the wet highway and the plaintive moans of ships cautiously threading their course through the fog. I strained to hear the sound of gravel crunching under a heel.

The gravel was cold on my face, and the dampness soaked through my shirt. On either side, the glow of the security beams filled the space between the piles with a ghostly light.

Without warning, a lengthy shadow fell on the ground between the two mountains of gravel. Moments later, a nebulous figure appeared, moving slowly, cautiously.

I cursed myself for leaving my .38 in the motel, but all I needed was to shoot someone else. What I had to do was mislead this joker. Get him moving away from me so I could disappear into the fog.

And I knew just how to do that very thing.

Moving as silently as possible, I rose to my knees and hurled a marble-sized gravel chunk at the distant pile of gravel, figuring the clatter would distract him long enough for me to slip away.

I missed the pile. Fact is, my rock bounced off the gunman's head.

"What the—" he shouted and grabbed the side of his face.

I bolted, half running, half falling down the mound of gravel and took off for the darkness beyond the office. Behind me, curses filled the night along with slugs from his automatic. I kept waiting for the impact of a slug, but none came.

Glancing over my shoulder, I saw only the fog behind me. If I could reach the beckoning darkness, I could cut across the yard toward the pickup.

I looked around just in time to see a figure before me, and then a shadow filled my vision.

THE NEXT THING I felt was a rough vibration against my back and a growling, grinding screech in my ears. I sensed movement, but the pain in my head scrambled any logical reasoning. I touched my fingers to my forehead and winced. I could feel a knot already starting to form.

I flung my arm out and slammed my knuckles into a wall of metal. I grimaced at the pain. Shaking my head, I stared into the darkness. I was moving, ascending, but…I closed my eyes, wanting to sleep.

Still groggy, I stretched my legs and struck another solid wall. Abruptly, my eyes popped open as my scrambled thoughts came together, making me realize the peril

I was in. I was riding in one of gravel buckets to the top of the silos. "Jesus!" I shouted, peering over the edge of the bucket. I caught my breath. All I saw was fog. I could be ten feet or fifty feet above the ground. I squeezed my eyes shut. I was still groggy.

Suddenly, the giant mixer came to life in a hubbub of grinding gears and screeching metal. Above the clatter of the belt and the falling gravel, I could hear the great blades begin scraping the inside of the mixer.

If I didn't get out of the bucket before it reached the top, I would be dumped with the gravel down into the mixer, becoming a somewhat disparate ingredient of Jerry Cook's slurry. I clambered over the side of the bucket, trying to find a spot for my feet. I perched on the thin frame of angle iron supporting the bucket.

With a clatter and bang, the fourth bucket ahead of me dumped its load. I breathed a sign of relief when I spotted an inspection ladder at the top of the silo. All I had to do was step off the belt onto the ladder, and I would be safe.

So I thought.

When I reached the ladder, I stepped onto a rung, but my light jacket snagged on a corner of the bucket, almost jerking me off the ladder. I wrapped my arms and legs around the steel frame of the ladder. The bucket moved inexorably toward the lip of the silo, pulling the jacket ever tighter about my shoulders.

My arms began to slip. With a loud groan, I redoubled my efforts, but I was no match for the powerful motor and gears driving the conveyor. Slowly, the pressure straightened my arms, scraping my forearms across the rusty rails of the ladder until I was holding only by my fingers.

I clenched my teeth and squeezed as hard as I could. My fingers began to straighten. "Hold on," I muttered grimly. "Hold on."

Suddenly, there was the sharp rip of nylon, and all of the pressure ceased. I clung to the ladder in relief, my breath coming in labored gasps. I remained motionless for several minutes, too weak to attempt a descent.

Then a familiar voice came through the fog. "Tony? Tony? Where are you?"

My voice was only a raw croak. "Virge?"

"Yeah. Where are you?"

"Up here."

"Up here, where?"

Shakily, I started down. "Never mind. Here I come." Virgil was looking up at me when I came out of the fog. "Where have you been?" I managed to gasp out.

He looked around warily. "In the truck, waiting for you. When you didn't show up, I came back to see what was going on. I got no idea where that mutt is. You find something up there?"

I leaned my forehead against the cold railing. I didn't know whether to laugh or cry.

"You all right?"

I pushed away from the ladder, my knees still shaky from the incident. "Yeah, yeah," I mumbled. "I'll live."

DURING THE RIDE back to the motel, I told Virgil what had taken place.

"Geez, Tony. I wish I'd knowed. I was sitting in the pickup all nice and snug waiting for you. When you went out the back door, I went out the front. I figured you was going straight to the truck."

For the first time since we broke into the office, I felt like grinning. "That's what I was planning on doing, but some bozo started shooting at me, and things went downhill from there."

Virgil grunted. "I don't know about you, but it looks to me that the cement company could be as deep in this diamond thing as Cheshire and the others."

The fog remained thick. I drove slowly, keeping my lights dimmed. The scary thing about driving in fog is that you never know exactly where you are. There's no warning, no hint of your location. One second, you're staring at a gray wall of moisture. The next, you're in the middle of an intersection with cars bearing down from both sides.

And that's how this whole case was turning out. I didn't know where I was, and people kept taking shots at me.

"What puzzles me, Tony, is where the cement company fits in," said Virgil.

I kept my theory about the cement truck to myself. "What puzzles me, Virge, is how any of this fits together. We know some diamond smuggling is going on, but there's no when, no definite who, no where, no why."

We drove a few minutes in silence. Virgil was pulling out a cigarette when I announced, "I think I'll pay Sam Maranzano a visit tomorrow."

Virgil bit through his cigarette. He shook his head. "From what I hear, Sam Maranzano don't like visitors."

"He'll like me."

IT TURNED OUT I was the one who had a visitor, and when it was over, I wished it had been Sam Maranzano.

ELEVEN

I ROSE THAT MORNING at 5:30 a.m. as usual, retrieved my complimentary morning newspaper while a pot of motel coffee perked, and went online to pick up my messages. After coffee and perusing the news, I went through my morning ritual of showering, shaving, and in general making myself presentable. I paused for a few seconds to grimace at the knot on my forehead, a gift from my unknown admirer only a few hours earlier.

Whoever he was, his message was unmistakable. *Stop the meddling.*

A knock on the door interrupted my musings.

"Come on in, Virge," I shouted.

The door remained closed.

With a frown, I jerked it open and froze.

Janice Coffman-Morrison, my on-again, off-again significant other.

She stood there like a fragile porcelain doll, wearing an ankle-length black leather coat. Her matching cap sported a long white feather that I knew to be a fake because of her animal rights campaigning. She stared up at me coldly.

I was surprised, and pleased, and puzzled. "Janice. What are you doing here? Come in. Come on in."

Without a word, she strode inside and stopped in front of the TV, staring at the wall. Closing the door, I followed after her. I laid my hands on her shoulders. "This is really a surprise. You shouldn't have bothered. Everything is going to be all ri—"

She spun on her heel and slapped the dickens out of me.

Her next words were not in the vernacular taught the rich girls in the most prestigious private school in Atlanta. Oh, no. The idiom into which she lapsed could be found on any street corner in any inner city. "You lousy, dirty…" Well, from there, she ticked off a few reprehensible characteristics of my ancestry.

I don't know which stunned me more, the slap or her virulent description of my character, some of which was probably richly deserved, but at the present—well, she had me confused.

However, I did manage a fairly sophisticated retort. "What the…"

Her eyes blazed. Her round little cheeks flushed with anger. "How dare you try to blame Ted for the trouble you're in. I've never heard of anything so shameful in all my life. Why, I can't believe you'd stoop so low, so cowardly. It's…it's the most…" She sputtered. Words failed her, so she slapped my other cheek.

I grabbed her wrists before she could get after the first cheek again. I've never been too enthusiastic about the cheek-turning business because all it ever got me was a blow upside the head. "What are you talking about? I haven't blamed your cousin for any of my problems."

She stuck out her pretty jaw. "That isn't what I was told."

I wanted to tell her that didn't surprise me, but she was already angry enough. "I don't know what you were told, but all I did was ask your cousin about an acquaintance of his. That's all."

She tried to jerk her wrists from my grasp, but I held tightly. "Let me go." Her voice rocketed an octave in those three words.

"Not until you promise to stop slapping me."

She glared up at me, her brown eyes like lasers. She pressed her lips together.

I held tighter. "Promise or we'll stand here all morning."

Her eyes softened slightly, and her lips relaxed. She gave a terse nod.

"All right," I said, releasing her wrists and stepping quickly back out of her range. "Now, what's this all about?"

"Ted said you were trying to put the blame on him for killing a policeman. The poor, sensitive dear is grief-stricken over such an accusation."

All I could do was stare at her. Finally, I shook my head. "I don't know where he came up with that idea. Yeah, a cop was killed. I told you about that. I shot him because he shot a friend of mine and was trying to shoot me."

From the skepticism in her eyes, I knew she didn't believe me. "That's not what Ted told me."

"When I talked to Ted last night at his apartment, I asked him what his relationship was with Frank Cheshire, the cop I shot." I left out the particulars about the diamonds and smuggling. The less she knew about that, the less trouble she could cause me. "Cheshire hired Ted to fly to Philadelphia and check with a buyer for some goods. Your cousin said he met Cheshire through a mutual friend." I didn't tell her the mutual friend was a bartender.

Janice eyed me suspiciously. "Why would Ted work for someone else? He works for a law firm."

It took a supreme effort on my part to keep from rolling my eyes. Ted Morrison was turning out to be a quite a liar—perhaps not too polished, but certainly prolific. I shrugged. "Maybe he had the extra time and decided to pick up a few extra dollars. I don't know. All I know is that was the extent of our conversation."

Our gazes locked. I didn't look away. I knew her well enough to know that if I did pull my gaze from hers, she'd believe I was lying. She'd grown up with her Aunt Beatrice and more than once, I'd heard her aunt proclaim that liars would never look a person in the eye.

Her gaze wavered. "Why would Ted tell me something that wasn't true?"

I relaxed somewhat. Her initial resolve was beginning to crumble. "Maybe he misunderstood. Maybe he was so upset that he just got the whole thing twisted around." It was a blatant lie, but in my job I had become an accomplished liar, and I could look anyone in the eye without wavering.

A tiny frown knit her eyebrows. "You think so?"

"Sure." I smiled warmly. "Happens all the time. I promise. Ted Morrison had nothing to do with the death of Frank Cheshire."

"Honest?"

"Honest."

Her shoulders sagged, and a deep sigh escaped her lips. Tears welled in her eyes. "Oh, Tony, I'm so relieved. I just couldn't believe that you of all people would think something so...so horribly terrible about Ted. Aunt Beatrice thinks the world of him. And besides her, he's the only living relative I have. Even though I haven't had a chance to spend much time with him, I would just die if anything happened to him. He seems so sweet."

Sweet was not the word I would use. "Well," I said, "put your mind at ease. He'll be all right."

She paused, collected herself, and shook her head in disgust at her behavior. "I should have known that you would never do anything to hurt him."

She could have gone the rest of her life without making that last remark. Janice Coffman-Morrison didn't know it at the time, but she had just placed me between the proverbial rock and the hard place.

After she left, ostensibly to spend some time with her only other living relative, sweet Teddy Morrison, I plopped down in a chair and stared at the table for several minutes. I already had plenty of problems, and now she had just dumped another little jewel in my lap.

Pouring another cup of coffee, I pulled out my note-cards and added the events of the previous twenty-four hours to them.

There was hard evidence that Cheshire and Allied Cement were at berth 21 that night. Less conclusive was the wingtip shoe I spotted at the base of the industrial Dumpster by the freshly poured cement. But I still had my ideas about it.

That was the night Albert Vaster turned up missing. I pondered the information. "Mustache Pete" Abban-dando had ordered Albert to follow Cheshire. Cheshire was on berth 21. An Allied Cement truck was at berth 21. I found a wingtip slipper on the dock near the fresh cement. And Albert Vaster wore wingtips.

I grimaced at the singular theory that popped into my head.

Was it possible that Cheshire killed Vaster, buried him in the fresh cement, inadvertently stepped in the cement, leaving an impression, then fired at Ben and me thinking we were with Abbandando's gang and had stumbled onto him?

Far-fetched, perhaps, but maybe not as far-fetched as it might actually be. Of course, there was still no hard proof. It was just a wild theory. Like they say, that and a buck will get you a cup of coffee.

A thought hit me. Something I'd forgotten. There was someone else there. I heard running feet. Morrison? I wasn't sure, but there was still something else about that night that bothered me.

The telephone rang. I eyed it warily, then lifted the receiver to my ear. "Boudreaux? This is Sergeant Wilson. Ben Howard has taken a turn for the worse."

Before I could stammer out a reply, he hung up.

Time was running out. If Ben died, the Galveston P.D. would in all likelihood throw my worthless carcass as deep into the jailhouse as they could.

Time to see Maranzano.

When Virgil asked me why, I replied with, "I don't know what else to do." That seemed to satisfy him.

THIRTY MINUTES LATER, Virgil and I turned off I-45 into downtown Houston, bound for the main office of Maranzano Enterprises.

Morning traffic was heavy, and we caught every red light along the way. "They ain't going to let us see Sam, Tony. I guarantee it."

I turned onto Main Street. "Let's wait and see, Virge. Can't tell about folks. Sometimes they turn out to be mighty accommodating."

MARANZANO'S BUTTON MEN didn't know the meaning of accommodating. "Boy," Godzilla's brother growled at me, "you got no business around here. Now beat it, or we'll beat you."

I grinned weakly at the square-jawed man glaring

down at me. "Okay. No problem for me. I'll just pass on Frank Cheshire's last words to the cops."

Square-jaw's eyes grew wide, then quickly narrowed. "Hold on, buddy." He waved over his shoulder and three hulking brutes stepped forward, each with a hand in his coat pocket. "Wait here."

I nodded. "Whatever you say." I decided to say nothing of the drive-by shooting a couple of days earlier in Abbandando's office. I wanted to see if Maranzano recognized my name. Stood to reason a man would know the name of someone he ordered wasted.

Five minutes later, Virgil and I were escorted into Sam Maranzano's presence. Two button men sat on the couch, one slight and bald, with eyes black as a shark's, the other twenty pounds heavier and sporting a scar from under the lobe of his left ear to his chin.

Sam Maranzano, a short, roly-poly man with a round face and thin strands of dark hair carefully combed across a squat head, frowned at me. "What's this about Cheshire's last words? What did he say about me?"

"Nothing." I shook my head and glanced at the frowning goombahs who had risen to stand behind Maranzano.

"That ain't what you told my boys."

"All I told them was that maybe I'd pass on Cheshire's last words to the police."

Maranzano eyed me suspiciously.

I continued. "Your boys just assumed he was talking about you."

"What'd he say?"

I grabbed at my heart. "Hey, I been shot."

He stared at me in disbelief. A faint grin curled his fat lips, then the grin faded into a puzzled frown.

I shrugged. There was no accounting for a person's sense of humor. "Well, Maranzano, the truth is, I was too far away to hear what he said. I just wanted to talk to you."

A smug, cat-ate-the-canary grin spread over Maranzano's pan-shaped face. "You're a dumb bird. You know what I can do to you?"

"Look, all I'm after is some information. What does that hurt?"

He held up two fingers forming a "V" above his right shoulder. The goon with the scar placed a fat cigar between Sam's fingers. "Go on."

I told him who I was and what had taken place over the last few days. If he recognized my name, he covered it well.

He grunted and eyed the cigar. "So, what information you want?"

"Was Cheshire working for you?" I didn't plan to tell him about the anonymous call from my mysterious cop connecting him with Cheshire on the smuggling caper.

He bit off the end and spit it on the floor. "You can't be stupid enough to expect me to answer that."

I laughed. "No. And I'm not stupid enough to come here without half of the Galveston Police Department knowing where I am."

He jabbed the cigar at one of his boys. "Show these two out, boys. Their time is up."

I waved the bald-headed goombah back. "Not yet, Maranzano. I got a couple more questions, then I'll beat it."

He sneered. "I can make you go. And never come back."

"I know, but I don't figure you want any heat because of me. I'm no threat to you...unless Cheshire was taking care of your business out at the dock the other night. If he was..." I shrugged.

Sam Maranzano studied Virgil and me as he touched a match to his cigar and blew a stream of blue smoke toward the ceiling. He nodded, my signal to continue.

The fact that he didn't order us to be measured for a new pair of shoes gave me some reassurance. I explained what had taken place at the dock. "I don't know what he was doing there. I think it was dirty, but I've got to prove it. If I do, then maybe I'm off the hook with the shooting."

"What about the cop you say Cheshire shot?"

"Ben Howard? He's in a coma at the hospital. He might not make it."

Maranzano grinned. "Tough. He croaks, you take the fall for offing two cops. Makes you antsy, huh? Kinda nervous, huh?" He laughed. I had the distinct feeling he was enjoying my predicament. He was probably the kind of kid who pulled legs off grasshoppers.

"I can tell you this: I don't sleep too well at night."

He roared. "I can see how that might be." He shook his head and wiped at the tears of laughter in his eyes.

Virgil and I exchanged looks. He arched an eyebrow. I just shrugged.

Sarcasm edged Maranzano's voice. "I could tell you I didn't have nothing to do with whatever he was doing out there. You wouldn't know if I was lying or not."

"Nope. Suppose not."

"So, why should I say anything?"

"You got nothing to hide, so why not? You're a smart man with a large organization. I don't figure you'd tolerate any loose cannons running around. And Cheshire was one."

The grin faded from his lips. He studied me a few more seconds. "Let me put it this way, Boudreaux. Frank Cheshire went where the money was best. I hadn't had no dealings with him for a year now." He eyed me levelly.

For some strange reason, I believed him. I gave him a brief nod. "Thanks, Sam. That's all I wanted to know." I tapped Virgil on the arm. "Let's go."

We turned and opened the door, meeting a wall of stone-faced goombahs who would have enjoyed pulling off our legs. Behind us, Sam grunted, and the goombahs parted.

I looked back. "If I was you, Sam, I'd watch my back."

He arched a wary eyebrow. "Yeah? Why's that?"

"Your name keeps popping up in this mess. A lot of

accusations are being tossed your way. I found from experience that if something is said long enough, someone's going to believe it."

"WHAT DO YOU think, Tony?"

I kept my eyes on the road. The traffic was thicker than last night's fog. "About what?"

"Cheshire. You think Maranzano's lying to us? You think Cheshire was working for that fat worthless bag of scum?"

I considered Virgil's question. "Could be, but I don't think so." Virgil frowned at me, and I explained. "There was no reaction from him when he learned my name. Now, if he'd put out a hit on me, he would have remembered, and he would have reacted somehow, but he didn't. He didn't even blink. I don't think Sam Maranzano has that kind of self-discipline."

Virgil screwed up his face in concentration. "He could be a good poker player."

I couldn't resist a grin. "Might be, but we've got to have a starting place. Let's say Maranzano is telling the truth. He hasn't had any dealings with Cheshire for a year. Why would the informant from the police station say he was? If Cheshire wasn't working for Maranzano, maybe that means he was working for himself."

"Or Abbandando."

I arched an eyebrow at Virgil's theory. "Yeah, or Abbandando. Maybe." I muttered a curse. I still had no hard evidence that Cheshire was dirty. Morrison was my one hope, and he refused. Even if I beat it out of him, he could always recant. It looked like I had to keep butting my head against the proverbial brick wall.

TWELVE

I-45 TRAFFIC TO GALVESTON was bumper to bumper, miles and miles of Texans jammed together, weaving in and out, back and forth, eighty-mile-an-hour spirits constrained by a fifty-five-mile-an-hour speed limit and caught up in a twenty-mile-an-hour traffic jam.

The mindset of Texas drivers is to follow each other as closely as possible, and regardless of speed, never leave enough room for another vehicle to slip into, or they will. And finally, with the cold resolve of an Old West gunfighter, Texas drivers abhor turn signals, believing there is no sense in giving the guy behind you any clue to your next move.

Probably the best description of Texas interstate traffic is that it is first cousin to chaos, confusion, and commotion.

City traffic is no better. I cut south on 61st Street to Seawall Boulevard, a broad, four-lane thoroughfare paralleling the beach fourteen feet below. A broad sidewalk with a high curb separated the boulevard from the drop-off to the beach.

If anything, traffic grew even more chaotic once we hit the boulevard.

I learned long ago the way to defeat the anger and

frustration of traffic was to stay five miles below the limit and let everyone pass. And pass they did, on both sides, front and back, and some idiots even tried to go over and under. Within a mile, I had more than two dozen different vehicles whip in front and then move on.

So I wasn't too concerned when a black Lincoln Town Car eased in front of me and slowed. I simply backed off the gas and held my distance.

He remained in front. Another guy who hates to fight the traffic, I told myself, noting that he had a passenger. We tooled along Seawall Boulevard at a steady 50 mph.

"Water's smooth today," Virgil mumbled, peering at the gray waves slurping against the sandy shore below.

"Yeah." I glanced out across the slick expanse of the Gulf of Mexico. Chances were we'd have another thick fog tonight.

From the corner of my eye, I noted another vehicle pull up beside us. I shot a quick look. A white Chrysler. The Lincoln remained in front.

Only a few pedestrians strolled the sidewalk.

Without warning, the Chrysler to my left slammed into us. At the same time, the Lincoln in front slowed. The passenger looked back at us.

Virgil grabbed for the dash. "What the—"

The pickup bounced over the curb and onto the sidewalk. I jerked it back, smashing into the side of the Chrysler and knocking it back into the middle lane. I shot the car a glance and spotted a face leering up at me.

The driver yanked his Chrysler into me again, trying to force us off the seawall and down to the beach below. I jerked the steering wheel to the left.

Metal shrieked and sparks flew. Traffic piled up behind us.

"Get us out of here!" shouted Virgil. "Honk at that guy to move."

I sped up, holding down the horn and hoping the Lincoln Town Car in front would move out of the way, but he slowed even more. "He's part of it," I muttered between clenched teeth.

Virgil cursed.

I couldn't slam on the brakes, I couldn't head down the sidewalk for fear of pedestrians, and I couldn't move left. I had only one choice, and I had to do it fast.

Ahead, I spotted a stretch of sidewalk clear of pedestrians.

Taking a deep breath, I slammed into the Chrysler, knocking it into the inside lane. Quickly I backed off to gain some distance from the Lincoln in front. In the next moment, I floorboarded my old truck. With a roar that sounded like a tornado, the powerful V-8 engine kicked in, and we shot forward, aiming for the left rear fender of the Lincoln.

If I hit him in just the right spot, I could knock the car into a spin.

The driver saw me coming and slammed on his brakes, too late. At the same time, the Chrysler shot toward me, hoping to pin my truck between the two vehicles.

Seconds before the Chrysler hit, I slammed into the Lincoln's fender, sending his back end spinning to his left. I spun the steering wheel sharply, slamming into the Chrysler and forcing him back into the inside lane.

I glanced in the rearview mirror in time to see the spinning Lincoln bounce over the curb, cartwheel across the sidewalk and plunge down the seawall to the granite below.

Moments later, a ball of fire ballooned into the sky.

The accident frightened the driver of the Chrysler. He sped away, but I was right behind him, saying a small prayer of thanks for not trading in my old truck for a shiny new one.

I'd had this old truck for years. The body was ragged, but the engine and running gear was pure precision. Like the old man's brag, there might be snow on the roof, but there's fire in the furnace. That was an apt description of my truck. A hundred-dollar body wrapped around a two-thousand-dollar engine. Other than a few little $70,000 sports cars, there was not a vehicle back in Church Point, Opelousas, or Lafayette that could stay with my truck.

The Chrysler was running like the proverbial turpentined cat, and I was right on his tail, moving closer with every turn and twist he made. I'd forgotten about Virgil. I glanced at him. "You okay, Virge?"

He nodded, jaw set and thick fingers digging into the dash so he wouldn't roll all over the seat. "Get that sucker."

Traffic was holding our speed down, but once or twice, I managed to nudge the back of the Chrysler's fender and almost send him into a spin. The driver was bent over the wheel. His passenger was slamming his fists against the dash and glancing back at us frantically.

Abruptly, we broke out of traffic.

Immediately, the Chrysler shot up to over a hundred miles an hour.

I could have followed, but I reminded myself that my mother had not raised a fool. Besides, I had the license number, not that it was legit. I backed off, back down to the speed limit.

Moments later, the Chrysler tried to take a corner too fast. He slammed over the curb, through a palm tree, and went into a long, bouncing roll that literally sent pieces of metal flying in every direction, tearing the vehicle apart before it exploded.

I pulled up to the curb and raced to see if I could help, but I was too late.

Two of the officers who answered the call had been at the hospital that morning I went to see about Ben. They would have probably hauled my carcass to a back room and interrogated me without mercy had not an off-duty officer shown up. I recognized him also from the hospital.

"Hold on, guys," he said. "I saw it all." He looked at me and froze. Finally, he muttered, "You."

"Yeah. It's me." I braced myself for the worst.

He muttered a curse and shook his head in frustration. "Look, guys, as much as I hate to say it, Boudreaux here isn't to blame. Two cars tried to run him off the road. I saw the whole thing from behind. Only some fancy driving on his part stopped them." He gestured to the burning car. "When this old boy sped away, Boudreaux backed off."

The two officers stared at him. "Come on, Jack. You know what this guy did to Ben Howard and Frank Cheshire."

Jack glared at me. "One's got nothing to do with the other. I want to nail his worthless hide for what he did to Cheshire and Howard, but this isn't his doing. It wasn't his fault."

All I could do for a moment was gape. Maybe there were some good cops out there. "Thanks, buddy."

"Don't thank me. It's my job. I'd do it for anybody."

VIRGIL AND I gave our depositions at the station. As we were leaving, the same two uniforms who had covered the accident met us downstairs. One jabbed a thick finger at my chest. "We're patient, Boudreaux, but you can bet we're going to nail you to the wall."

Given the opportunity, of that I had no doubt.

Virgil grinned wryly as we climbed into my old pickup. "You got an odd assortment of friends here," he said, nodding to the gray brick exterior of the station.

"Oh? You just noticed, huh?"

We both laughed, but it was strained. I had the feeling the walls were beginning to close in. That meant I had to kick one of them down.

And the first would be the one behind which Albert Vaster lived.

I didn't try to explain my reasoning to Virgil. How do you explain feelings, nebulous hunches based upon someone's body language or word inflection? You don't. If you're desperate, you just act on them.

Thinking back to my visit with "Mustache Pete" Abbandando, I recalled that the obese crime boss wasn't even sure that Albert was following Cheshire that night. He just thought his cousin might have been following Cheshire. For all he knew, a jealous lover might have offed pretty-boy Albert and dumped him in Galveston Bay.

I had my own theory now, but first, I wanted to find out if Albert knew about Cheshire and the diamonds. And the only way I could start learning about Abbandando's younger cousin was by searching his apartment. Without any interference. That meant I had to break into it.

"JEEZ, TONY. YOU'RE taking some kind of chance," Virgil warned me when I told him what I had in mind.

"Not so much. Abbandando says he wants me to find out what happened. So, I'm out there looking."

My heavily muscled bodyguard shrugged his massive shoulders. "You count on Pete for backup, you're still asking for trouble."

"Maybe, but we're going in circles. If there's something there, I've been too dumb to see it."

He shook his head and leaned back in the seat. "Whatever." He remained silent for a few moments. "Hey, that was some fancy driving out there today. I mean, bouncing the guy in circles. How'd you learn that?"

"Believe it or not, I spent a couple thousand on a week-long professional driving course in Austin. Same one the cops go through. Truth is, I never thought I would use it."

He chuckled. "Well, you done good."

EVEN AN AMATEUR could have opened Albert Vaster's door in less than thirty seconds. It was a matter of inserting a couple of picks, making a couple of twists, and bingo, we were in.

I don't know if you'd call the apartment classy, but it was expensive. Carpet that you sunk to your ankles in, leather furniture, glass tables, a TV that almost filled one wall, and a hot tub in the bathroom.

Virgil grunted. "Poor guy. Looks like he had to struggle to just get by."

I arched an eyebrow at his wry comment. "Yeah. Okay, you take the bedroom. Any kind of paperwork, pictures, brochures about anything. Specifically, I'm interested in shipping lines, dates, anything that can give us an idea when the shipment is due."

"If there is a shipment," he said, eyeing me skeptically.

"Yeah." I grimaced. "If there is a shipment."

I glanced around the apartment. There were no desks, so I started at the kitchen counter, where I uncovered an assortment of unpaid bills and receipts from restaurants, gyms, and the IMAX movie out at Moody Gardens.

Muttering curses under my breath, I went through every drawer, every cabinet, every catalog, every book. And found nothing.

Then I started in the living room, flipping through telephone books, digging in wastebaskets, looking under cushions.

Virgil emerged from the bedroom. He had a single slip of paper in his hand. He shook his head and handed me the folded sheet. "This is all I found. It was in one of his coat pockets. A bunch of numbers and letters."

I unfolded the slip and frowned as I stared at a puzzling set of numbers and letters. *1-146-1-21, ccc, bp, 1-22.* I read it aloud to Virgil. "Make any sense?"

He shrugged. "Not to me. Except maybe that '1-21' or '1-22' could be dates."

"I hope not," I replied, arching an eyebrow. "That's yesterday and today."

Virgil grinned sheepishly. "Yeah."

"This all you found?"

"Yeah. No magazines, no books. All he must've done in that bed was sleep."

I folded the paper into my pocket. We spent another fifteen minutes tearing the place apart and finding nothing.

When I opened the door to leave, I came face-to-face

with Augie of the red hair. Two scowling button men stood behind him, hands jammed in their pockets. Augie stared at me coldly. "Pete wants to see you."

THIRTEEN

His BACK RIGID as a steel bar, "Mustache Pete" sat in a wingback chair, dressed in a white silk suit and looking very much like an albino pear. His pencil-thin mustache accented the grim twist on his lips as Virgil and I, like recalcitrant children, stood in front of him while I explained my visit to Albert Vaster's.

"There were too many loose ends. I figured I might tie up a couple at your cousin's apartment. Perhaps find a hint to where he might be." I added the last remark for Pete's benefit. I was more interested in Cheshire than Vaster.

Curling his fat fingers and touching them to his shiny vest, he said. "You could have come to me."

With a casual shrug, I said, "It was no big deal. No sense in bothering you when I could pop in and out in fifteen minutes." I hoped my insouciant aplomb convinced him that my visit to the apartment was of little importance. And as far as I knew, it had been—depending on the meaning of that eclectic collection of numbers we had discovered.

He dragged the tip of his tongue over his fat lips. "What did you find?"

I laughed. "Nothing. Not a scrap of anything. I'm

right back where I started." I kept silent about my theory regarding the fate of Albert Vaster. I might be wrong, and right now I couldn't afford another problem. The D.A. was giving me all I could handle.

"Mustache Pete" studied me intently. I knew he didn't believe me, but he had nothing to prove otherwise. I settled the question for him. "Anything I run across about your cousin, I'll let you know. Anything."

As WE DROVE away from the warehouse, Virgil snapped his fingers. "Hey, those numbers…if they got to do with shipping, why don't we just ask somebody around here? They ought to be able to tell us."

I lifted an eyebrow. "Yeah, tell us and Abbandando, too. We can't take the chance. We've got to figure it out ourselves."

THE GALVESTON PUBLIC LIBRARY sat on the corner of Church and 23rd, its red brick façade showing nicks and ragged corners from the great flood of 1900. The Galveston Historical Committee had pressured the city into remodeling the interior in the 1950s and again in the 1980s.

Inside, Virgil and I sat around a table on which rested a stack of the *Galveston Daily News*. We skimmed through the current and following week's maritime shipping schedules, time in and time out for every vessel docking at each of the thirty-five or so berths along the north side of the island.

"Take a look. This could be our '1-22,'" I said, pointing to the date at the top of the week's schedule. "Today, Monday, January 22. This is the list of ships due in this week."

Virgil nodded, a crooked grin on his face. "That means the goods are coming in sometime this week, huh?"

I drew a deep breath. "Could be."

During the current week, there were thirteen ships due into port. Virgil read them off, and I jotted the names down on a notecard.

"We got three Centennial cargo ships, seven foreign ships, and three government ships."

Virgil pointed to the card. "What about the Centennial line? That begins with a C. Maybe the shipment is on one of those."

We had discussed the cryptic set of characters we discovered in Vaster's apartment only briefly. None of them made sense except maybe "1-22," today's date. However, none of the vessels were due to berth today. "Where's the three Cs?"

He shrugged.

I read the list of ships, the independents as well as the line ships. "*Centennial Texas, Centennial Maryland, Centennial California, U.S.S. Wilberforce, Marshall,* and *Robert Holly.* Now, the foreign lines. Two from Great Britain, the *Chauncey Meadows* and the *Liverpool.* Then there's the Seven Seas' *Falcon* from Spain, Tri Oceans' *Voyager,* Turkish Cargo Lines' *Allah*

II, Mauritania Royal's *Escort,* and Oceania Steamship Company's *Daniel Smith.*"

"I don't see no three Cs." Virgil growled.

I studied our situation a few moments. "We got a mountain here. Too much to wade through. Let's try to narrow it."

Virgil arched an eyebrow. "Easier said than done."

"Maybe not." I indicated the newspapers. "We'll go back two months and list all of the vessels and shipping lines that have berthed at the port here. Then we'll go online, check their current and future schedules and see what we come up with."

Frowning, Virgil looked at me blankly. "You can do that?"

"What?"

"Find all them schedules on the computer."

I gave him a crooked grin. "I don't know, but we're going to give it a try."

By SEVEN P.M., we had our list compiled.

Grabbing a bag of hamburgers and fries, we reached the motel by eight and went online.

We surfed for a few minutes, then finally stumbled onto the right links. Within another thirty minutes, we had a list of over one hundred and fifty maritime shipping lines.

Checking the list against the arrivals and departures from the Port of Galveston, we discovered eight shipping lines that regularly berthed there.

I read back over the list. Of the eight, four of the shipping lines were scheduled to berth in Galveston during the week: Seven Seas, Turkish Cargo Lines, Centennial Cargo, and Oceania Steamship Company. There was a fifth line scheduled in—not a regular. Tri Oceans Lines.

"You think the shipment is on one of them?" Virgil was looking over my shoulder.

I shook my head and blew out through my lips in frustration. "I got no idea. If those Cs mean anything, I don't see it."

Suddenly Virgil blurted out. "Hey. Look at that." He pointed to one of the shipping lines on the master list. "Centennial Cargo. Didn't we see some vessels coming from Centennial?"

I glanced over my notes. "Yeah. *Centennial Texas, Centennial Maryland,* and *Centennial California.* So?"

His voice shook with excitement. "*Centennial California.* Centennial Cargo *California.* Three Cs."

I caught his enthusiasm. "Could be. Centennial Cargo *California.* Three Cs." I scanned the schedule, searching for the cargo of the vessel. I frowned when I found it. "General cargo." No telling how many tons of general crap they would be bringing in. Everything from Taiwanese towels to Manchurian mud flaps.

Finding a cache of diamonds in that mess was like matching two snowflakes. Of course, if I were smuggling diamonds, that's exactly the type of cargo I would select.

"You think that's it, Tony?"

"It looks good, Virge. Still…" I spread my notecards on the table.

"What are you doing?" Virgil frowned, puzzled.

"Hoping to spot something that doesn't belong. Something that sticks out. Yet nothing in particular. The *California* might be the one we're looking for. And it might not."

"Huh?"

I grinned. "Sometimes if you spread notes out like a picture, sort of rearrange them, you'll spot something you've overlooked. Maybe there's another three Cs in here somewhere."

He eyed me skeptically. "If you say so."

As soon as I laid them out, I spotted it.

The *Voyager,* owned by Tri Oceans Steamship Lines. I remained calm. "There it is, Virge."

Virgil grunted. "What is?"

"Tri Oceans. Look at it. Tri means three. Three oceans or seas—c,c,c. That could be it, too."

He shook his head and raised a skeptical eyebrow. "Kinda stretching it, huh?"

I ignored his skepticism. "Take a look at the list of arrivals and departures for the last couple of months. What about Tri Oceans Lines? You see them?"

Slowly, Virgil studied the list. Finally, he shook his head. "No." He looked at me, confused. "Why?"

I jabbed my finger at the schedule. "A Tri Oceans vessel, the *Voyager,* is due in the 26th." I paused and considered the matter. "I wonder where it will berth? In fact,

I wonder where each of them will berth." I grabbed the telephone and dialed information for the Port of Galveston.

I frowned when the dispatcher informed me that Tri Oceans' *Voyager* would berth at 23, but the frown turned into a grin when he told me the *California* would berth on the 24th, two days from now, at berth 21.

Berth 21, on the same pier where I ran into Cheshire, the same pier that Abbandando's stevedoring firm used, the same pier where the last patch of cement had been poured.

I leaned back and grinned sappily at Virgil. There are coincidences, and then there are coincidences.

"What?"

"Virge, old buddy. I think I got it figured out."

"Well, let's hear it."

"I'm guessing Abbandando is behind the caper. The *California* berths at his dock on the 24th."

"What about the rest of the letters and numbers?"

I shrugged. "Well, I'm not sure, but I think that at least we've made some headway."

Virgil arched an eyebrow.

Before I could say another word, the phone rang. I answered it and froze.

"Boudreaux. This is Sergeant Wilson. You better get down to the hospital. Looks like Ben Howard is dying."

I sat gape-mouthed, staring at Virgil as the dial tone hummed. Virgil leaned forward. "Tony! What—"

A knock at the door interrupted him. He held up a

hand to stay me as he headed for the door. When he opened it, Ted Morrison staggered in and collapsed. He looked like someone had fed him through a meat grinder.

AFTER ASSURING MYSELF Morrison wasn't going to croak in my motel room, I left him with Virgil and raced to the hospital. Raced might not be the word, for the fog was thick. Crept is better. I cursed Galveston and its January fogs.

I felt nauseous. I couldn't believe it. Ben Howard— dying. I remembered some of the cases we'd worked together. He was irascible, but a good man to work with. Like the old cowboys used to say, he was one to ride the river with.

There was the time we chased a killer through the darkened backyards of a ritzy neighborhood at night and all of us, killer and all, ran into a swimming pool. That was the night we not only solved a year-old murder, but blew away a gang of drug dealers who had been selling to high school students.

Despite the fog, traffic was heavy. While I had pretty well neglected my religious upbringing the last few years, I mumbled a short but sincere prayer for Ben. Naturally, I was worried about my own skin, but for one of the few times in my life, I was more concerned about someone else than my own hide.

Half a dozen uniforms were clustered in the ICU waiting room. Sergeant Wilson was waiting in the doorway for me and quickly ushered me down the hall. "This is no time to be around those other boys, Boudreaux," he announced, interrupting my questions about Ben as he backed me into an empty room.

"But how is he now? What's going on?"

He grimaced. "I don't know for sure. They lost him for—"

"Lost him? You mean..."

"Yeah. He died, but they got him back. We haven't heard nothing from the doc yet, so we don't know what's happened."

I closed my eyes and breathed a sigh of relief. "Thank God."

Wilson grunted. "Yeah." He glanced briefly down the hall in the direction of the ICU waiting room, then looked back at me. "How are things going with you?"

I studied him a moment, wondering how honest I could be with him. On the one hand, I wanted to lay out all I had, and get feedback from another lawman. But on the other, what if he was just a plant for the D.A.? After all, he compromised no one when he told me he that the D.A. was going out of his way to build a case against me. Of course, he didn't say District Attorney, but that's who he meant.

Yet he had found Ted Morrison's address for me.

Neither effort was enough to warrant taking a chance on him. "How's it going? I don't know, Sergeant. It's kinda like back home, paddling across a bayou. You got alligators all around, just waiting for you to flip over."

"You need anything?" He glanced nervously in the direction of the waiting room.

"Yeah. Who knows the most and the worst about Galveston? Every city has one."

His eyes widened in surprise, followed by a knowing grin on his face. "There's an old broad down at the *Galveston Daily News*. Lela. Lela Hoffman. She's been down there sixty years. Nothing goes on in this town that she doesn't know about."

At that moment, a hospital staff member in green scrubs entered the ICU waiting room. Wilson excused himself. "Be right back."

A couple minutes later, the uniforms departed, grinning and joking. I relaxed. Wilson returned, nodding and grinning. "He's stable."

"They know what caused it?"

His grin faded. "No. It was unexpected."

I closed my eyes and shook my head. "That means it could happen again."

Wilson arched an eyebrow. "Hey. Be positive about this situation. It could happen, but it won't. Get me?"

We studied each other a moment. A faint smile curled my lips. "I got it. Thanks."

OUT IN THE PARKING LOT, I climbed into my old pickup and called Virgil. Morrison was conscious. Nothing appeared busted or broken. But he was scared.

I figured anyone who was well enough to be scared

wasn't about to croak, so I stuck him on the bottom of my list of things to do. First, Lela Hoffman.

Then I realized the time. 10:00 p.m. Only the night shift would be at the paper. Hoffman would be home. I could catch her there, but then I remembered Wilson's remark, "she's been down there sixty years." Sixty years? She must be at least eighty. I shook my head. She was probably in bed at six every night. I'd catch her in the morning.

Reluctantly, I headed back to the motel. During the drive, I called Austin, and my boss, Marty Blevins. I needed to bounce my theories off someone, and that someone was Al Grogan, the top sleuth in Marty's stable of P.I.'s. Al had helped me more than once. I always figured that maybe he was somehow genetically related to the fictional Sherlock Holmes, for his intuitiveness constantly surprised me.

I was about to hang up when Marty answered. His voice was terse, irritable. That puzzled me at first, for he never hit the sack before midnight. Then I understood. Marty perceived himself a ladies' man. And as long as the tequila held out, he played the role. Every time he left the office to pick up his date, he held up a bottle of cheap tequila and said, "One tequila, two tequila, three tequila, floor," then leered lecherously. So apparently, he had found the floor once again, and not by himself.

I apologized and gave him a way out. "Marty. This is Tony. I didn't mean to wake you."

A raspy but feminine voice sounded behind him, too

muffled for me to understand. I grinned to myself. I was right.

"Hey, Tony. Naw, naw. You didn't wake me." He hesitated and covered the mouthpiece, but I could hear him. "In a minute. Pour us another tequila." His voice grew loud once again. "I was just laying here…ah…reading a book, you know? What's up?"

I quickly explained my situation.

Marty was apologetic. "Sorry, kid. Al's in Cancun. Just left. He'll be out for two weeks. Can I help?"

"Yeah," the feminine voice said. "You sure can." Wicked little giggles punctuated her remark.

I couldn't resist a grin at his predicament, but I knew I could trust Marty, and that was about all I could say. He was a plodder, a lot like me. Two of us would probably get nowhere twice as fast in half the time. But at least I could get someone else's reaction.

"Okay, Marty. I'll e-mail you what I have and what I think. Put your spin on it. Maybe you'll spot something I've missed."

FOURTEEN

TED MORRISON WAS sleeping fitfully when I came in. His torso had so many welts and knots that if you painted it red, it could pass for the Martian landscape. I studied the welts. There are welts, and then there are welts. Welts form in the shape of the instrument causing them. I had seen welts like these before in the interrogation room, where rogue cops used batons and slappers for some extracurricular activity. I nodded to them and cocked an eyebrow at Virgil.

He shrugged. In a hushed tone, he said. "Says Maranzano's boys did it."

"Why?" I had a couple of theories, but that's all they were. Theories. But the truth was, Maranzano wasn't part of them.

"No idea. Claims he never had any dealings with Maranzano."

That made no sense. A family member screws the pooch, then expect retaliation. But, roughing up someone for no reason, someone outside the family—that made no sense.

"You believe that, Virge, and I've got lakefront property in the middle of the Sahara to sell you. Wonder why he came here?"

Virgil arched an eyebrow. "Maybe you're the only one he trusts."

"I doubt that. He knows I know about him and Cheshire. I just can't prove it. Not yet. And he won't admit it."

"What do you want me to do with him?"

At first I didn't understand Virgil's question. "You mean for tonight?"

"Yeah. Want me to take him to my room?"

"No sense in that." I shook my head. "Let'm sleep. I'll take the other bed."

Virgil rose and stretched. "You sure? I'm ready to hit the blankets."

I agreed. "It's been a long day. Yeah, just leave him here. I'm going to take a shower and then send out some e-mail."

After closing and bolting the door, I headed for a hot shower. I was tired and sore, but all in all, I had managed to accomplish a great deal. Enough, I hoped, to give me some direction for tomorrow.

Morrison appeared to be sleeping soundly. I still had trouble with Maranzano being behind the beating. I padded into the bathroom and turned on the shower. As in many motels, a door separated the vanity and shower facilities.

I failed to close the door completely. Steam from the shower seeped into the vanity and sink area. I noticed I was out of soap, so I climbed from the tub and opened the door enough to grab a fresh bar of soap.

I froze.

Ted Morrison was reflected in the mirror. He was on the floor, beneath the dresser, against the wall.

Stepping back inside quickly, I climbed silently into the shower and hastily soaped and rinsed. I snugged my robe about me and returned to the bedroom. Morrison appeared to be sleeping on the bed, in exactly the same position as when I'd left the room.

My mother raised no idiots. I acted as if I had good sense and went about my business. I booted up the computer and put together my e-mail for Marty Blevins.

Just before I finished, Morrison awakened. With a pitiful groan, he climbed from bed and hobbled to the bathroom. The door clicked shut.

Instantly, I dropped to my knees and fumbled up under the dresser. I cursed as I jammed my fingers into its solid wooden underbelly. I stretched far back and ran my hand up the back of the dresser. My fingers stiffened as I touched a plastic bag taped to the back of the dresser. I ripped it off and jammed it in a pocket.

The commode flushed. I jerked back, scraping my arm across a sharp corner. I ignored the pain and slipped into my chair just seconds before Morrison reappeared.

He hesitated, glanced at me, and managed a weak grin. "Thanks for letting me stay here tonight."

"Not to worry. You look worn out. Get some sleep. We'll talk in the morning."

He nodded gratefully and climbed back into bed.

I sat at the computer, typing gibberish while my heart thudded against my chest. What was going on here?

Obviously, you dummy, he's setting you up for someone, I thought. The cops, most likely.

I hoped the single packet was all he planted. Then I remembered his visit to the bathroom. Just as he pulled the covers up about his neck, I rose quickly. "Uh oh," I said. "Nature calls."

I didn't bother to close the door. I glanced behind the commode. Nothing. I flipped through the stack of towels.

Bingo. Another bag. About a hundred dollar's worth. Same as the other. I ripped both bags open and dumped them in the commode and flushed it, watching two hundred dollars of nose candy swish down into the sewer. Just to be on the safe side, I flushed it a second time.

Back in the bedroom, I worked on my e-mail to Marty. My heart was pounding so hard, I knew Morrison must've heard it. As my adrenaline slowed, my anger rose. I bit my tongue and finished my e-mail. With a final punch on a button, I sent it into cyberspace.

Then I looked at Morrison, who appeared to be sleeping.

I was about two seconds away from breaking one of his knees when a loud knock sounded at the door.

"Boudreaux! It's the police. We have a warrant. Open up."

Morrison sat upright, his eyes wide in feigned surprise.

I eyed him coldly, and I saw the recognition in his

eyes. He knew I knew what he had done. He licked his lips nervously.

The cops pounded on the door. "Boudreaux!"

"Hold it, hold it," I yelled. "I'm coming."

When I opened the door, three brawny uniforms burst in. One jammed a warrant in my hand. "Illegal drugs. Sit down. Don't move."

I obeyed without protest, which surprised them. Obviously they had anticipated some argument on my part.

One tore through the vanity and then disappeared into the bathroom. Another yanked and grabbed at the clothes in the closet. A third rummaged through the drawers, pulled the dresser from the wall, and peered behind it. A puzzled frown flickered over his face. He gave Morrison a fleeting look, but Morrison was glancing desperately at the door.

The one from the bathroom reappeared, a puzzled frown on his face. "Nothing," he muttered, shooting Morrison an angry look.

"Nothing here, either," replied the second and the third.

I rose slowly. "Sorry you made the trip for nothing, boys." I shook my head and clucked my tongue. "I've noticed that we're getting a mighty inferior quality of stool pigeons this year."

If looks could kill, I'd have died right there.

They glared at me, then exchanged puzzled looks, uncertain as to what they should do next.

Abruptly, Morrison jumped out of bed and slammed

the heel of his hand into the chest of one of the uniforms. "What do you think you're doing, coming into a man's room like this? You got no right."

The outburst surprised all of us, but a second uniform reacted quickly. With a shout, he grabbed Morrison around the chest and spun him away.

One of the officers shot a threatening look at me. I held up my hands, shook my head, and backed away in time to see Morrison take a wild swing at the uniform who had seized him.

Instantly, all three pounced on Ted Morrison, cuffing his hands and screaming obscenities at him.

All in all, I thought they were putting on a good show, probably better than the made-for-TV movie Channel 3 was showing.

"You're going down to the station, buddy," one shouted, shoving Morrison toward the door.

With a startled grunt, Morrison stumbled against the end of the bed and fell forward roughly, banging his head against the open door. He jerked around, a thin line of blood appearing on his forehead.

One of the uniforms cursed. "Come on. Let's get him out of here." He glanced at me. I saw a flicker of alarm in his eyes. I just shrugged.

Virgil was standing outside the door when it opened.

Ignoring him, the three blueboys ushered Morrison down the gallery.

His eyes questioning, Virgil paused in the open doorway and watched as the small procession disappeared around the corner. He looked around at me. "Looks like you had some excitement."

"Morrison was a plant. Two bags of happy stuff. D.A. must have sent him. You notice the welts on him?"

Virgil frowned. "What about them?"

"I've been thinking about them. I've seen enough 'persuasion' in the back room to recognize welts raised by batons. They must have worked him over good before he got here."

"Huh? They? The cops? That don't make no sense. Why work him over if he's on their side?"

I arched an eyebrow. "Maybe he isn't on their side. Maybe he honestly has no idea what's going down. Maybe."

"Oh." Virgil nodded slowly. "I see." He hesitated and shook his head. "No. I don't see."

A few pieces were beginning to fall into place. I hoped it was because that was where they belonged rather than because I wanted them to fit. "Morrison could be on the level. Cheshire could have hired him as a courier of sorts—feel out the fence, do the legwork."

Virgil snorted. "Huh. I don't know. I think he's neck deep in the whole thing." He paused, then said, "Before you got the call about Ben Howard, you were saying something about the Centennial Cargo and Tri Oceans lines. You got something figured out on them?"

For a moment, I stared at him, confused. So much had taken place in the last few hours, I'd forgotten about the vessels. But now I remembered. "Yeah, yeah. The

California. Where are my notecards? I'll show you what I'm talking about."

Once again, I spread the notes and printouts. "The *California* is a regular at the Port of Galveston. All these other lines are regulars, too, except for Tri Oceans. Now, I'm making some far-fetched presumptions here, but look at what we have. First the note, '1-21, ccc, bp.' What if the '21' is the berth. That's Abbandando's. Second, 'ccc' could be Centennial Cargo's *California* or Tri Oceans' *Voyager*."

He arched a skeptical eyebrow. "Okay, but what about the other numbers and the letters 'bp'?"

I gave him a wry grin. "Beats me."

He tapped his meaty finger on the list of vessels. "So how do we know which is which between the *California* and *Voyager*?"

Smuggling goods was a new game for me, but it stood to reason that a cache of diamonds would logically come from a country that produced diamonds, or at least, the seaport nearest that country. To my fairly naive understanding of smuggling, I figured chances were less likely that diamonds would come from Cuba rather than from South Africa or Australia. "I'm guessing, Virge, that we should focus on the vessel that had a port of call in a diamond-producing country."

He eyed me skeptically. "But what if they deliberately sent the goods to another country to bury the trail? That's what I'd do."

I studied him a moment. "Don't confuse me. I got all I can handle with this."

He drew a deep breath and nodded to the printouts on the table. "You know where the ports of call were?"

"If I don't, I can get them." I thumbed through the printouts. "Centennial Cargo's *California*'s last port of call was Abidjan on the Ivory Coast. She's loaded with general cargo."

"You figure the shipment came out of there?"

I pondered his question. All I'd heard about Abidjan was that whatever your taste, you could get it there. I nodded. "A shipment of hot diamonds coming out of the Ivory Coast wouldn't surprise me." I looked back at the printout and grimaced.

"What about the other vessel, the *Voyager*?"

"Yeah. There's plenty on it. It'll berth at 23, remember?"

Virgil nodded. "Where's it been?"

I flipped through the printout until I came to the schedules. I whistled when I spotted the *Voyager*'s ports of call. "Freetown, Sierra Leone."

"So?" Virgil frowned at me.

"So, Sierra Leone is home to probably half the world's known diamond mines."

Virgil's eyes grew wide. "Half? Did you say half?"

"Well, maybe not half, but there's enough there that we can't afford to overlook it, or the *Centennial California*."

"Okay, so now we have two ships that could be bringing in the diamonds. My next question is how we find out which one."

I sighed. "I got no idea. Not now." Suddenly, I was exhausted. One second I vibrated with energy, the next I felt like every ounce of strength had been drained from my muscles. "I'm beat, Virge. I gotta get some sleep."

BUT SLEEP DIDN'T COME. I lay awake for over an hour, sorting, cataloging, trying to make the pieces fit. Logically, the vessel with the diamonds would berth at Abbandando's. That was the *Centennial California*. Even if I were right about that, I had no idea in what guise they would attempt to bring the diamonds ashore.

A familiar thought started nagging at me, one I had experienced in every investigation, one I tried to ignore, but one that continued to batter at me. What if the basic hypothesis was flawed? What if there were no diamonds at all? What if shooting Ben Howard was a mistake? What if Albert Vaster was not buried in cement?

Somewhere in all of the "what ifs," I finally drifted off to sleep.

That night I dreamed of being strapped on the execution gurney at Huntsville Prison. Ben Howard inserted the needle into my arm.

FIFTEEN

THE MORNING DAWNED bright and clear.

After a shower and fresh cup of coffee to clear the cobwebs from my head, I felt better. Not much, but somewhat. I had two vessels, the *California* and the *Voyager,* both anchored offshore awaiting a pilot to bring them in. The *California* was due the next day, the *Voyager* a couple of days later. I didn't have much time to discover just how the diamonds would be brought ashore. To compound the problem, I hadn't the slightest idea where to begin.

I remembered Lela Hoffman. I reached for the receiver, then hesitated. What if I was just wasting more time, time that was growing more valuable with each passing second? What could she provide me?

With a wry grin, I muttered, "I couldn't be any worse off than I am now." I dialed information.

Occasionally, I meet someone who truly surprises me. Lela Hoffman was one of those. Her answering machine took my message after informing me that she would soon return from her morning tour of the island on her Harley.

An eighty-something on a Harley? I chalked it up to fun-loving mischief with an answering machine until

I received a call sometime later from Lela Hoffman. I heard breakers crashing on the beach in the background. "This Tony Boudreaux?" she asked. Before I could reply, she continued, "Got your message. Do I know you?"

"No." I told her of my meeting with Sergeant James Wilson. "When I told him I wanted to talk to someone who knew the best and worst of Galveston, he told me to get in touch with you."

"You a reporter or what?"

From the tone of her voice and the way she spoke, I had the feeling this wasn't a senile old broad I could spin a yarn on. "Nope. Private investigator. Out of Austin."

"Austin? Ain't we got no P.I.s in Galveston that we got to go to Austin for one?" Her voice was demanding, the words shrill with a hint of sardonic humor.

I didn't know how to answer, so I stuttered, "Well, I'm...I'm sure...ah...sure that you do. It's just that I don't know anyone around here that I can get a straight answer from."

"How do you know you can get it from me?"

"I don't."

She chuckled. "You a looker?"

"Beg your pardon."

"Are you good looking?"

I decided two could play the game. "Ugly as sin."

"Oh." Her tone sagged in disappointment. "Well, I got no time today. My schedule's full. This is my morning to tour the city on my bike. I'd give up sex before I'd miss my rounds of the city."

Sex? At eighty-something? I couldn't resist laughing. "I sure wouldn't want you to give up sex. When do you think you will be free?"

"Don't know." Then she said, "You a bike rider?"

"More or less."

"Skinny or fat?"

"Skinny."

"Tell you what. I'll pick you up. You can ride around the city with me, and we'll talk."

I was speechless, a reaction I seldom experience.

She must have taken my silence for consent. "Where are you?"

Without thinking, I replied. "Sea Gull Motel. On…"

"I know where it is. Be there in five minutes. Wait out front for me." She spat out her words like a machine gun and then hung up.

I replaced the receiver and shook my head, wondering just what kind of mess I had myself in now.

Virgil wasn't too keen about being left behind. I explained, "No way we can all fit on a Harley, Virge."

"I can follow in my car. Something happens to you, Blevins will be on me like a thick coat of ugly."

I cocked an eyebrow at his skewed analogy. "I'll be fine. Trust me."

LELA HOFFMAN WAS right on time, and certainly not what I expected. Instead of a little old gray-haired woman putt-putting into the motel parking lot, a diminutive figure in black leathers and a helmet with a black visor dipped sharply into the parking lot, roared down the drive, braked abruptly, and slid to a halt six feet from me.

A gloved hand flipped open the visor and an animated face smiled at me through the wrinkles framed by short tufts of gray hair. "Boudreaux? I'm Lela Hoffman." Her light blue eyes sparkled.

She stuck out her hand, and I took it. I wondered if I should shake it or kiss it, but her quick, firm grip gave me my answer. I shook it. "Yeah. Tony Boudreaux, Ms. Hoffman."

Arching an eyebrow, she looked me up and down like she was inspecting a side of beef. With a nod, she said. "You are a looker. Call me Lela. Now grab the helmet on the sissy bar and hop on the bush pad. I'll show you our fair city."

I climbed on and immediately wondered what I was going to hold on to. The top of her head came to my chin. "Grab my waist, but don't let your hands roam," she instructed.

"Yes, Ma'am," I replied, grinning at the back of her helmet.

"Leave the visor up. I'll go slow so we can talk. And I promise, no catwalks."

"Catwalks?" I frowned.

"Yeah. You know, wheelies."

I gulped and held on to her waist desperately.

THE WAVES CRASHED against the sandy beach as we headed down Seawall Boulevard. The acrid odor of gasoline and exhaust mixed with the tang of salt air.

Lela gave me a running account of the history of the massive concrete wall that protected the city from the treacherous storm surges of threatening hurricanes.

We pulled up to a light. "But, you didn't call me for a history lesson," she abruptly announced.

"No."

"So?"

I blurted out. "So, a cop got killed four nights ago. Guy named Frank Cheshire. I was told he was dirty. I need proof."

She turned her head and gave me a sidelong glance. "You think I know?"

"I asked Sergeant Wilson who knew the best and worst of the city. He gave me your name. I want to hear all the rumors and gossip about dirty cops. Who they were, who contacted them, who paid them. Anything you can think of."

The light changed, and we sped away. "You don't want much," she called over her shoulder.

"Not much," I yelled back.

"I could make some people awfully angry."

"They'd get over it."

"Not the ones I know."

The population drops drastically in Galveston during the winter, permitting leisurely touring of the city along the palm-lined boulevards, past the imposing mansions, down the narrow lanes.

Lela started her narrative in the 1950s era, when the city had begun promoting tourism. "In addition to the community spirit, the city's determination, there was always an underworld presence," she said. "Hidden, never discussed. But it was there." And for the next hour, she embellished her story by pointing out the various sights and landmarks from Pelican Island to the Strand and to the tall ship, *Elissa*.

Finally, she pulled into a McDonald's and cut the ignition. "It's coffee time," she announced, leaving her helmet on a mirror. I put mine on the sissy bar and followed her inside.

Everyone from the hamburger flippers to the smiling cashier spoke and waved to her. She led the way directly to a booth against a wall of glass overlooking Galveston Bay. Moments later, two coffees arrived.

"They know you, huh?" I grinned at her, noting her short-cut gray hair and twinkling blue eyes that seemed to be peering deep inside me.

"Lord, yes. I've been coming here for years. Amazing how much gossip you can pick up here."

"Tell me about Sam Maranzano."

She shrugged as she poured cream and spooned sugar into her coffee. "Not much. He came along after I retired."

"I thought you were still with the news."

"Oh, I am, but only twenty or thirty hours a week. No more of those sixty- and seventy-hour jaunts."

Eighty-something, and she called twenty or thirty hours a week retired. I hoped I could retire as graciously. "I see."

"Yeah, but I keep up with things. Maranzano is the

new boy on the block. Takes care not to move on to Abbandando's turf."

"Abbandando's that big."

She laughed, and her eyes twinkled. "Literally, yes, figuratively, no."

I grinned at her humor. "He is porky."

She snorted. "You're being generous. He's so fat you could show the cinemascope version of 'Gone with the Wind' on the seat of his pants."

We both laughed. She continued. "No, Abbandando has ties back east. An uncle, Joe Vaster, who has his finger in every dirty pie you can name: drugs, prostitution, numbers...you name it, he has it."

"Vaster? I've heard that name before. Albert?"

She sipped her coffee. "Abbandando's cousin. He came down here sometime back. I figured old man Vaster wants his son to keep an eye on Fatso."

Suddenly, one of my theories picked up some support. "Abbandando is wanting to move out on his own?"

"That's what I heard. Then little Albert shows up."

"Cheshire work for Abbandando or Maranzano?"

"Both of them. He was like a ping-pong ball. You never knew who was paying him."

"How much of that goes on?"

"You mean, how many cops are dirty?" She shook her head. "Not many. Galveston is a good department, but there are some bad ones. It's that way everywhere." She hesitated, nodding slowly. "Some high up, very high up, but then that's where the real temptation is—not the nickel-and-dime stuff a beat cop gets."

I hadn't touched my coffee, too caught up in her animated revelations. "Can you give me some names?"

She gave me a sly look. "Nope. But, I'll do you one better. Find the political action committees that support the elected officials. See who's on them. You'll have your answer."

Political action committees? I frowned momentarily, then it struck me—elected officials, the sheriff, District Attorney, judges. I chided myself. Why hadn't I thought of that? "Yeah. Yeah, I see what you mean."

She pushed her empty cup away and started to rise.

"One more question."

Pausing halfway from her seat, she frowned, then slowly sat back down. "Just one."

"How about a date tonight?"

Her frown vanished. We both laughed. "You couldn't keep up with me, sonny," she replied, giving me a lewd wink.

EDDIE DYSON WAS my information man. A reformed stool pigeon, Eddie developed an affinity for the Internet just short of blood kin. Thanks to his exorbitant charges, I had been forced to develop my own search skills. Though they could not begin to compare with Eddie's, they served me well back at the motel.

As Eddie had told me earlier, because of the Internet, there were no longer any secrets. You just needed to know how to find the information.

I pulled up a search engine, typed in "George Briggs Political Action Committee," and within twenty seconds was staring at a list of donors to his last campaign.

The first name hit me between the eyes. Allied Cement. I scrolled down the list. I stopped at Maritime Shippers, Abbandando's company. I whistled. Virgil looked around from the John Wayne B Western on TV.

I clicked on Abbandando's company. My mouth dropped open and then a slow grin closed it. Lela knew what she was talking about, I told myself, as I read aloud the name of the donor. "Peter Abbandando." In the next column was the amount donated: $100,000.

Scrolling down the list of political beneficiaries of Maritime Shippers, I was rewarded with a list of all candidates who had received donations. Three of them, all councilmen, had received $50,000 each for the previous year's campaign.

Hastily, I called up Allied Cement.

I was not surprised that Director Jerry Cook had also donated $100,000 to Briggs and $50,000 to each of the other three councilmen.

With heavy donations like those, Briggs, Abbandando, and Cook had to be sleeping in the same room, if not the same bed.

Suddenly, a panorama of limitless possibilities spread out before me.

A couple of days earlier, after discovering the coke

Briggs had ordered planted in my room, I came to the conclusion that Briggs wanted to bury me deep in Huntsville to protect someone or something. At the time, I had no idea exactly what he was protecting, but from what I had learned since, there were half a dozen possibilities, ranging from bribery to—well, maybe even diamonds.

If Briggs was so desperate to protect whoever or whatever, then perhaps he might even take that extra step: murder. That would explain the drive-by attempt and the three goons on the dock that night. It could even explain the shooter out at Allied Cement.

I studied the PAC donor list. This had to be the relationship to which Lela Hoffman was alluding. The way it looked to me was that Abbandando, Allied Cement, and George Briggs could pass for the world's first set of Siamese triplets.

I skimmed down the list of PAC's, searching for more donors to Briggs. One donor looked familiar: British Paint Company. I'd never heard of it, so why should it seem familiar?

A dozen different scenarios raced through my head. This information had tossed a wild card into the deck, and all of a sudden, it looked like time for a reshuffle.

SIXTEEN

I PULLED OUT MY notecards and for the hundredth time began rearranging them. The process is similar to brainstorming in that by juxtaposing the cards, different ideas can be stimulated, some germane to the subject, others completely irrelevant.

Several fruitless minutes passed as I studied each new arrangement. Suddenly, I froze, staring at the card describing the wingtip slipper. Next to it was the card from the first night, the night I heard running feet just before Cheshire went on his shooting spree. A couple of pieces of the puzzle fell into place. I stared at the cards in disbelief, wondering how I had managed to be so dense.

"Whatcha see, Tony?" Virgil had scooted his chair around to face me. "Find something?"

"Maybe. I think maybe I did. Something that I had been missing all along."

He frowned at the notecards. "So?"

I paused to gather my rearranged theories. "Okay. Now, there's a lot of holes here, but bear with me. Maranzano says Cheshire isn't on his payroll. Maybe not, but Cheshire learned about the diamonds from somewhere. I figure Maranzano because I got a call from the police station. The caller claims Cheshire and Maranzano were in a smuggling caper together. But Cheshire took it a step farther. He and Morrison were planning a double-cross. They were going to hijack the diamonds from Maranzano. Someone else was out there that night, I mean besides Ben and me. I heard running feet. We also know that a fresh patch of cement was poured on Abbandando's pier that night."

Virgil shrugged. "Where you going with this?"

"What if Abbandando and Cheshire were in the caper together to double-cross Maranzano? And what if Albert Vaster got wind of their collaboration?"

The light of understanding brightened in Virgil's eyes. "You mean…"

"Yeah. Now I know this is pure conjecture, but I think there's a good chance that Albert Vaster is buried in the new concrete berth at Abbandando's."

Virgil's eyes bulged. "What?"

"I believe Abbandando helped get rid of his cousin."

"Why would he do something like that?"

"Good question. Now answer me this. What would it take to put away your own blood kin? How about millions in uncut diamonds? Now here it is. Abbandando was in the hijacking scheme with Cheshire. Albert stumbled on to his scheme. It stands to reason Albert would contact his old man back East because of the possibility of a gang war if Maranzano discovered Abbandando's duplicity."

"Okay. I got you."

I continued. "Abbandando had Cheshire off the boy,

called his friend Cook to bring in a load of cement, and they buried the one guy who could ruin them."

"Who's the Cook dude?" He paused. His eyes lit up. "That guy at Allied Cement?"

"The very one. He is also the Director of the Allied Cement Political Action Committee, a committee that donated a hundred thousand big ones to George Briggs' campaign last year for the District Attorney's office. Both Cook and Abbandando donated a hundred Gs."

It was Virgil's turn to whistle.

"You know," I added, "I don't believe Briggs set me up because of the shooting. I think he just doesn't want me nosing around."

"Could be." Virgil arched an eyebrow. "Could be. But, what's Briggs' part in all this? If he's responsible for what you say, what's he got up his sleeve?"

I shrugged. "Greed makes a person go to extremes. Maybe that's it." For the first time, I put my feelings into words. "Maybe the diamonds. Maybe something else."

"Sounds kinda iffy to me."

He was right. It was iffy. I had absolutely nothing to focus my theories, simply a conglomeration of half-baked ideas without a foundation.

A knock at the door gave me that foundation.

TED MORRISON STOOD sheepishly in the open doorway, his pale face purple and yellow from bruises. "Tony."

I held my temper. "You got some more dope to plant?"

He shook his head. "I'm sorry about that."

Virgil came to stand behind me. He sneered. "Yeah. We can see the tears."

I thought about Janice, which helped me resist the urge to slap Morrison senseless. On the other hand, I was going to be in enough trouble with her anyway when this hit the fan. A sound beating wouldn't elicit that much more yelling from her. "What do you want, Morrison?"

He dropped his gaze to the floor and shifted from one foot to the next. "I just wanted to apologize. That's all. I got nothing against you. They made me."

Virgil caught his breath.

"They?" My senses became alert. A tiny spark of hope burst into flame. "Who's they?"

He glanced nervously over his shoulder. "Can I come in?"

I hesitated.

He grinned sheepishly. "Honest. This is legit. I got nothing up my sleeve."

Virgil and I stepped aside to let him pass. Inside, he stood nervously in front of the TV.

"Looks like you fell down a couple times after you left here," I said, commenting on the bruises on his face.

He laid a finger on a yellow bruise near his cheek-bone. "Yeah. They was pretty upset that you stiffed them."

"Who's they?" I held my breath, wondering just how far Ted Morrison was prepared to go. I still held out hope that he'd testify for me.

He glanced at the closed door. "Look, the reason I'm

here is that I'm blowing this place. I got a feeling some-one's measuring me for a cement jacket, so I'm outta here. But I ain't leaving before they get what's coming to them."

Virgil and I exchanged puzzled looks.

Morrison continued, "I don't know all the details, but Frank Cheshire claimed the D.A. and Abbandando was thick as thieves."

So I was right. But that didn't make me feel any bet-ter. Worse, in fact. If the District Attorney was dirty, there was no way I could clear my name by proving Cheshire dirty. I managed to croak out a question. "In what way?"

He shrugged. "I never heard for sure, but all I know is that they was planning on hijacking a shipment of diamonds that belonged to Joe Vaster and lay the blame on Sam Maranzano."

I caught my breath. Joe Vaster! He was big time.

Virgil raised an eyebrow. "So Maranzano was tell-ing the truth. He wasn't mixed up in this."

Morrison's allegations had knocked a couple of holes in my theory. "Looks that way," I replied, at the same time realizing that there was a good chance the phone call from police headquarters concerning Cheshire and Maranzano had been a deliberate attempt to mislead me. "What else?"

Morrison shook his head. "That's all I know except Frank and me was planning on switching the shipment before handing it over to Abbandando and Briggs."

I eyed him narrowly. "They hired Cheshire to pick up the goods?"

He nodded nervously. "Yeah."

"And he planned on switching it on them?"

Morrison shrugged. "Yeah."

I whistled softly. "But the shipment was initially intended for Joe Vaster."

"Yeah. Through Abbandando's warehouse."

"How were you going to manage the switch?"

"Frank never got around to telling me."

"How was Vaster to make the pickup?"

He shrugged. "I don't know."

Virgil looked up at me. "You think maybe his kid was the pickup man, Tony?"

I shook my head. A plate of spaghetti didn't have as many loose ends. "Who knows, Virge? Who knows?" I looked back at Morrison. "When is the shipment due?"

"Frank never told me." He paused, looking from Virgil to me. "That's it. That's all I know."

I have a tiny voice somewhere deep in my head that tells me when something is, as Shakespeare so eloquently put it, "rotten in the state of Denmark." I didn't hear that tiny voice, but I was still suspicious of Morrison's motives. "Why are you telling me this?"

He pointed to his bruised face. "Call it my way of getting some revenge. After the cops finished working me over, I realized how far I was in over my head. I got scared." He glanced at the closed door. "I'm scared now."

I arched an eyebrow. "How'd you end up working with the cops to begin with?"

Morrison shrugged. "After Frank got it, they paid me a visit. I'm guessing Frank mentioned me to Abbandando, and from there it went to the D.A. He probably sent the cops for me. They found a kilo of coke in my apartment. That's the pressure they used to get me to plant the stuff in your room." He looked me squarely in the eyes. "It was me or you. I'm sorry."

I nodded. "Will you go to court with me? Testify for me? We not only take care of Cheshire but Abbandando and Briggs, to boot."

He shook his head emphatically. "No way, man. I never been as scared as I am right now. All I want to do is go someplace far away where I can start over, where nobody knows me. This ain't the kinda life I want."

"You could be subpoenaed."

He smiled sadly. "Sorry, Tony. I'd change my story."

I took my last shot. "Abbandando might come after you."

A wry grin curled his lips. "I never met Abbandando. You're the only one who knows this part of the story." He hesitated. "For fifteen years I've hustled, thinking I would score big and end up driving a fancy car. But I got nothing to show for it. I finally got smart and figured there must be a better way. My way sure ain't worked. I know what kind of crud I am for letting you down, but I just won't risk it. I'm sorry."

The truth is, I understood what he was saying, and

slapping him senseless wouldn't help, nor would toss-
ing him to Abbandando.

He paused at the door and looked back. "You probably don't believe what I've told you. Just to let you
know I'm on the up and up, I ain't a cousin or nephew
to those two broads in Austin. That was another scam."

His announcement surprised me. "But the DNA tests?
I know Beatrice Morrison. I know how exact she is."

He opened the door. "Maybe so, man, but there's always a way." He gave us a sly look and explained. "I
just supplied a family sample of DNA and bribed the
technician."

TEN MINUTES AFTER Ted Morrison left, the phone rang.

"Boudreaux? This is Wilson, Sergeant Wilson. I'm
trying to run down Ted Morrison. Seen him lately?"
His voice was thin and weak. He was on a cell phone.
I glanced at the window overlooking the parking lot
where I had met him a few days earlier.

Warning bells went off in my head. "Not since last
night."

He paused a moment. "Oh. Not this morning, huh?
Figured you two might have hit it off."

I had the eerie feeling that James Wilson was toying
with me. "Why would you think that?"

"No reason. You met with him a couple times, and
if I'm not mistaken, he is the cousin to a lady friend of
yours."

Though his remark took me aback momentarily, I

ignored the comment. "Like I told you. He was here last night when some of your guys came to my room with a search warrant and took him away." I hesitated, then decided to see what I could get from Wilson. "If I see him, is it important for him to get in touch with you?"

Wilson hesitated once again. "No. Don't worry about it. No big deal."

I sat staring at the receiver several seconds after I hung up. There was no question in my mind that Wilson suspected Morrison had paid me a visit.

"What's the matter, Tony?"

"I'm not sure, Virge. You remember when you were a kid and got into trouble? You mother would question you about it although she already knew the whole story. You know?"

With a chuckle, he nodded. "I know."

"That's exactly how I felt talking to Wilson. I got the feeling he knew Morrison had been here. So why the questions?"

"Maybe Morrison shouldn't of been here."

Virgil's remark gave me a idea. "Yeah. Yeah, and why shouldn't he have been here?"

"Huh?"

"I think you're right. What possible reason could Wilson have for Morrison to stay away from me?"

A broad grin split Virgil's square face. "So he wouldn't tell you what he just told you."

I grinned back at Virgil. "I think you're right, Virge. I think you just hit the proverbial nail on the head." I paused, suddenly aware of the ramifications of our new little theory. I frowned.

Virgil's grin faded. "What now?"

"If we're right, this means Wilson is in the scheme with Briggs and Abbandando."

"Yeah," Virgil replied, plopping down in a chair. "Makes you wonder just how many are involved."

My stomach growled.

Virgil grinned. "Me, too."

I looked out the window. The sky was gray, and the north wind blew spray off the whitecaps in the gulf. I shivered. "This is a day for gumbo, Virge. You ever had Louisiana gumbo?"

"I don't know about Louisiana, but we got a gumbo soup here."

I grinned to myself. Louisiana gumbo is to soup as a standing rib roast is to a Vienna sausage, but I just nodded. "Sort of."

"Let's get some."

Had I been back in my own apartment in Austin, I could have whipped up a tasty gumbo, but I had learned the hard way that Texas gumbo was a thin, watery imitation of a truly delectable dish. "I'll settle for a hamburger and fries."

We took Virgil's car, a new Pontiac Grand Am. I stared out over the gulf as we headed down Seawall Boulevard, trying to decide on my next step now that Morrison had bailed out on me. Whatever it was, I had to move fast. The first vessel, the *California,* was due in tomorrow.

"Drive-thru okay with you, Tony?"

"Huh?" I looked up. Ahead was the Seawall Hamburger Shack.

"I said is the drive-thru okay."

"Sure. No problem."

Five minutes later, we were headed back toward the motel. Traffic was typical for midafternoon. As we passed 26th Street, an eighteen-wheeler with a bright yellow trailer pulled up to the corner and stopped. In the middle of the trailer was a green paintbrush. I glanced at it idly, then turned my eyes back to the front.

Suddenly, I stiffened. The paintbrush!

I jerked around and stared out the rear window at the truck. Across the side of the yellow trailer was a bright green logo of a paintbrush. Above it were the words "British Paint Company" in bright green Britannic Bold font—the same as the unopened can of paint that I had seen under the kitchen sink at Frank Cheshire's apartment.

"Virge!"

He jerked around when I shouted. "What the…"

"Hurry. Back to the motel!" I yelled.

He frowned at me. "What's up?"

My voice trembled with excitement. "I think I just found our answer. If what I think is on the list of political action committees, I'll know where to find the diamonds."

I LEANED BACK in satisfaction. British Paint made sizeable contributions to the same candidates as did Maritime

Shippers and Allied Cement. "That is no coincidence, Virge," I said, pointing out the donations. "None at all."

"Now what?"

With a mischievous grin, I looked up at him. "We're going to find us a stash of fake diamonds. Let's go. We'll take my truck."

He looked at me as if I was crazy.

The truth was, I was saner than I had ever been.

SEVENTEEN

I TOOK THE STAIRS two at a time to Cheshire's apartment on the third floor. Once inside, I went directly for the kitchen. Virgil tagged after me, taking three steps to my two.

"Where are you…"

His voice trailed off when I opened the cabinet door under the sink. I looked inside and froze.

There were the same bug sprays, the same trash still overflowing and growing even riper, but only one can of paint, the one that had been opened and then taped shut. Traces of red paint had dried on the rim of the can. The second can, the unopened one, the British Paint can, was missing.

I dropped to one knee and cursed.

Virgil bent at the waist and stared under the sink. "What?"

"A can of paint is missing."

He looked around at me with a frown. "Huh?"

"There. Next to the red paint. There was another can there. A yellow one. British Paint Company."

The frown on his face deepened.

I continued. "The other day when we were here, there was a can of British Paint under here. It's gone now."

"So?"

"So, British Paint was a big contributor to the District Attorney last year. What easier way to smuggle in a shipment of diamonds than in a paint can?"

Virgil scratched his head. "I don't understand."

"Simple. Say a local vendor imports a shipment of British Paint for distribution to its stores. In that shipment is a single can filled with diamonds. By whatever means, Cheshire learned the location of the can, so he picked up an identical can and filled it with fake diamonds."

"Not bad. Probably the stevedore working the hold is in this with him. Takes the can, makes the switch, then goes about his business."

"Yeah, leaving Joe Vaster hanging and Abbandando with a handful of glass."

Virgil frowned. "But who could have known the can was here, in Cheshire's apartment?"

I arched an eyebrow. "Morrison."

A frown wrinkled Virgil's broad forehead. "I thought he was leaving town."

With a wry grin, I replied. "I'm sure he is. He just forgot to tell us when."

"What's our next move?"

"Sea View Plaza."

"Morrison's place."

"Yeah."

SURPRISE, SURPRISE. THE apartment showed no evidence that Ted Morrison was packing to leave town. And surprise, surprise again. There was no trace of the British Paint can.

Standing by the counter and peering up into the open cabinets, Virgil shook his head. He looked around at me, frustration etching lines of disgust in his rugged face. "Maybe Morrison ain't part of it, Tony. He's a wimp, and he seemed awful scared to me. Too scared to mess with Abbandando and that bunch."

I surveyed the apartment once again. There were only so many hiding places for a gallon-sized can of paint, and we'd searched all of them. "Maybe."

Virgil grunted and reached for a glass. "I bet he wasn't the one who took the can."

Frowning at my good-natured bodyguard, who was drawing a glass of water, I wondered. Who else would know about the fake diamonds? Abbandando? Briggs? No. They were the ones Cheshire was double-crossing.

"If not Morrison, then who, Virge?"

He looked at me blankly, holding a glass of water in his hand. He blew out through his lips and shook his head. "Beats me." He turned up the glass and in three great swallows gulped it down. "I got no idea," he added, setting the glass on the counter.

I muttered a curse. "Morrison was the one."

"What's this?" A sharp exclamation from Virgil caused me to look back around. He was studying a clear object between his thumb and forefinger.

"What's what?"

"This. It was in the kitchen sink." Suddenly, his eyes

grew wide. He looked at me in disbelief. "Tony. This is it. This is what we were looking for." Before I could reply, he blurted out. "It's a diamond."

For a brief moment, I was speechless. I groaned. Surely I hadn't screwed up again. The diamonds were already in. I closed my eyes in frustration. I stuck out my hand. "Let me see."

I studied the diamond in the palm of my hand.

"Is it real, do you think?"

Nodding to the empty glass, I replied. "Give me that. We'll soon see." Mentally, I crossed my fingers as I drew the diamond down the side of the glass.

Nothing. No scratch, no scar. I studied the diamond facsimile. The drinking glass had worn one corner from the imitation diamond. It was nothing but a cheap replica. A surge of exultation washed over me.

My theory was right. Move over, Sherlock Holmes. Make way for Tony Boudreaux. Morrison had the can of fake diamonds. Somehow, he was going to make the exchange. Or at least attempt to make it.

But how? Who was his contact? And what kind of plans had Joe Vaster made to pick up his shipment?

I shook the imitation diamond in Virgil's face. "We're getting close, Virge. We're getting close." I clenched my jaw in determination.

He grinned. "How close?"

"Close enough that all we have to do now is find out which of the two ships, the *California* tomorrow or the

Voyager later on, has a shipment of British Paint on its manifest."

Virgil arched a skeptical eyebrow. "How do we go about doing that?"

I headed for the door. "Where else? The computer. At least for a start. We'll take a look at their cargo manifests. If that doesn't work, we'll do it the old-fashioned way."

"How's that?"

"Legwork."

With a grunt, Virgil closed the door behind him. "I was afraid of that." He hesitated. "Tony?"

"Yeah?" I glanced around at him.

"What if there ain't no shipment of British Paint?"

I glared at him. "Don't say that, Virge. Don't even think it."

"BLAST!" I RESISTED the urge to slam the computer mouse against the pad. Last time I had given in to such an urge, I had to buy another mouse.

"No luck?"

I looked around at Virgil. "No. I can't get through to the manifest of either vessel. I guess we'll have to go down to the port and see what we can dig up."

Virgil cleared his throat. "I ain't no expert, but where does this British Paint come from? I mean, where is it put on the ship?"

"I don't see what that—" My words stopped abruptly as the point of his question became clear to me. "Yeah.

Yeah, I see what you mean. Find out which vessel made that port of call." I slammed the heel of my hand against my forehead. How simple.

I pulled up my favorite search engine, typed in British Paint, and presto, the British Paint website. At the bottom of the home page, a trailer proclaimed the factory was in Liverpool, England, which made that city the logical shipping port.

Next I pulled up the port of call manifest for the two vessels. With a groan, I stared at the screen. Both vessels had put in a week apart at Liverpool. That didn't help us.

Virgil stared at the screen. "The *California* is due in tomorrow."

"It's probably waiting offshore now."

"Probably."

I considered our situation. "I don't suppose you have a cousin who's a stevedore for Maritime Shipping, Abbandando's place."

"Sorry," Virgil replied. "But I do have a nephew who takes the pilot boat out to the vessels."

"That's something." I leaned back in the chair and studied Virgil. "Any ideas how he could get me aboard the ship?"

He considered the question a moment. "Not a chance. Besides, it's probably a container ship."

"Container? What's that?"

"You know, those large aluminum containers they load straight off the ships onto the eighteen-wheelers."

"Well, then that means we've got to take care of it when it berths."

"Got any ideas how to do that?"

"Not exactly, Virge. But, it'll come to me. Here's the way I see it. Morrison has the can of fake diamonds. Obviously he plans to switch them with the real ones. I don't know if he'll do it on board or later. I'm guessing later because I can't see him and Cheshire involving a third party."

"Yeah, but wouldn't it be easier for them to have a third party on board?"

"Maybe, but there's a security risk. What if the third party decided to see what was inside? He could pull a switch on them. They wouldn't discover the switch until they opened the can. No, I think they planned to wait until it was unloaded, then make the switch."

Virgil nodded slowly as he sorted through the scenario. "Right out in plain sight of God and everyone, huh?"

I chuckled. "Yeah."

EIGHTEEN

THE CLERK AT the East End Hardware rang up my purchase of a gallon of British Paint, a pint of paint thinner, and four panes of window glass.

"What's the glass for?" Virgil asked when we climbed back in my pickup.

"Diamonds."

He frowned, then a small grin tipped up his lips.

BACK AT THE MOTEL, we used a funnel to pour about half the paint into an empty three-liter soft drink container, filling it three-quarters full.

I placed the paint-filled bottle at the end of the vanity.

Next, we had to make our diamonds, which we did simply by shattering the glass and dumping it in the can, filling it to the brim. We then refilled the can with paint and tapped the lid down snugly. Using the paint thinner and towels, we wiped the excess paint from around the rim of the lid. Several quarts of paint still remained in the three-liter bottle. I poked some toilet tissue in the neck.

I shook the can. It rattled. I grinned at Virgil. "Instant diamonds. Now, all we have to do is figure out how to make the switch." I paused and glanced at my notecards stacked on the desk. On the top card was the set of enigmatic numbers and letters, "1-146-1-21, ccc, bp, 1-22."

Picking up the card, I indicated the first five digits. "The secret is right here, Virge. We know 21 is the berth, but the rest, well, I don't know how to go about breaking it. We can't ask anyone at the dock. They might get suspicious."

"There's always the Seaman's Center."

I frowned. He explained. "Sort of a YMCA for seamen new in port. You know, a place for them to go and relax, shoot a little pool, chew the fat."

In an instant, his point became clear. "One of them might know what the numbers mean."

"Could be."

"Even if they don't, at least we have it narrowed down to the *Voyager* and the *California*. Both are due in this week and both fit the three Cs."

"I been thinking, Tony." Virgil cleared his throat. "With Cheshire out of the picture, Morrison has to move fast. I don't think he can afford to wait until the container is off-loaded."

Virgil's theory made sense to me.

As far as we knew, Abbandando and Briggs knew nothing of Morrison. They would be making plans to move the container into the warehouse. Morrison would have to get to the container ahead of them. "Since we don't know where the diamonds are, our surest bet is to stake out the dock and see if Morrison is going to make a play."

Virgil grinned ruefully. "Yeah. Wherever he goes, there's the diamonds. If I was Abbandando, I'd unload that container first."

"Let's hope Morrison beats him to it."

"And then we'll follow Morrison and wait for the opportunity to make our switch."

"Yeah."

"What if he don't give us the chance?"

I shook my head. "He's got to. A guy walking off the dock with a single can of paint is too obvious. He'll stash it somewhere." A sudden thought hit me. I grimaced.

"What?" Virgil frowned up at me.

"You know, if we hang around the docks long enough, someone might get curious."

"Maybe not."

"But if they do, then what? We need some kind of identification that says we can be there."

Virgil thought a moment, then grinned. "No problem. Why don't you make us a couple visitors' passes on that computer of yours. Stick 'em in those clear plastic name-tags. Nobody'll pay no attention."

I stared at him. What a slick idea. I slapped Virgil on the shoulder. "What would I do without you, Virge?"

"And overalls," he added. "Blue ones. You know, like uniforms."

All I could do was shake my head at his inventiveness.

A visit to the local discount house supplied both our

needs, blue overalls and tags. Back at the motel, I printed up two cards with the word "visitor."

I rose and stretched, working the kinks from my muscles. "You hungry?"

"Yeah, now that you mention it. Where do you want to eat?"

"I'm too beat to go for a ride. How about the restaurant downstairs? In the morning, we can give the Seaman's Center a shot. Maybe someone there can tell us what the numbers mean."

Virgil rose to his feet, rolled his massive shoulders, and nodded. "I gotta go to my room first. Wait for me."

I started to protest, but I was too tired. "Okay. I'll call the hospital. See how Ben is."

Virgil left and I dialed the hospital, muttering a silent prayer that Ben had come out of the coma. I wasn't quite sure just how all this diamond business was going to clear me of the shooting, or if it would.

I spoke with the nurse on Ben's floor. No change.

Disappointed, I replaced the receiver.

Virgil pounded on the wall. I pounded back and headed for the door.

I opened it and gaped at two surly thugs standing on the gallery in front of my door glaring at me, each with an automatic in his hand. Instantly, I slammed the door, catching one of the goons' hands between the door and jamb. He screamed in pain and dropped his automatic.

Then another bellow sounded outside the door.

Virgil!

I yanked the door open.

Virgil had slammed his shoulder into one thug, driving him back into the second. I had no idea where the other automatic was, but I figured I might as well join the fight. I ran at the second thug, slamming my hands in his chest and shoving him over the gallery railing.

With a wild, terrified cry, he flipped head over heels and landed on top of a new Mustang convertible, crushing it down into the seats. In the meantime, Virgil and the first thug were pounding away at each other.

I kicked the thug in the back of his left knee. His leg collapsed, and as he fell, Virgil caught him in the side of his head with a fist the size of a cantaloupe.

We rolled him under the railing and off the gallery, but as his legs slipped off, he had enough presence of mind to clutch the edge of the gallery sidewalk.

He dangled in midair. I proceeded to stomp on his fingers, and he crashed to the ground.

He stumbled to his feet as his partner struggled out of the crushed ragtop and staggered into the drive. Caught up in the exhilarating fervor of our victory, I looked around for something to throw. I grabbed the plastic bottle containing what was left of the paint.

At that moment, headlights appeared at the end of the drive. A Lincoln Town Car slid to a halt, and the two thugs yanked open the doors. I heaved the bottle of paint at them.

If I had deliberately tried a thousand times to put

the bottle inside the Lincoln, I could never have done it. This time, it sailed through the open front door and slammed into the floorboard. The impact uncorked the tissue paper in the neck and geysers of yellow paint sprayed out in every direction.

Amid loud curses, the Lincoln sped away, the partially blinded driver bouncing off half a dozen parked vehicles before reaching Seawall Boulevard.

Several tenants ran outside at the commotion. One glanced up at us. "What happened?"

I glanced at Virgil and grinned, then looked back down. "Some idiot came barreling through here in a Lincoln and hit a few cars on the other side of the parking lot."

Virgil chuckled. He appeared unhurt after the brawl.

I patted my stomach. "I'm still hungry."

"Me, too," he replied. "Me, too."

THE RESTAURANT HAD a ubiquitous seaside motif, resplendent with palm trees, nets, and life rings with "*U.S.S. Albatross*" printed on them.

In the manner of old-time gunslingers, we sat against the back wall, facing the door.

Over a dinner of fried shrimp, soft-shell crabs, and fried potatoes, we tried to figure out just for whom the two thugs worked, Briggs or Abbandando, or both.

Between bites of shrimp, Virgil said, "If we believe Morrison, both those jokers were behind it."

I had to agree. Tonight's encounter was a level above

previous encounters. It was one thing to plant coke, but quite another to come armed. "I have the feeling, Virge, that our guys are getting nervous."

"You figure they heard we talked to Morrison?"

I nodded emphatically. "Well, Sergeant Wilson could have passed word to Briggs, who in turn informed Abbandando. If that's the case," I added, quickly checking out the two couples entering the restaurant and making their way to a table by the front window overlooking Seawall Boulevard. "Then Abbandando knows we're aware of the diamonds. But what they don't know is that we know how the diamonds are coming into the country." I grinned at Virgil. "That's our advantage."

"But we don't know when," he added.

I frowned at him. "Don't go throwing cold water on things, Virge."

He chuckled.

As I LAY IN BED that night with my .38 under my pillow, I realized that any advantage we thought we had was strictly in our minds. Briggs and Abbandando could take us out at any time. Morrison was the only hard proof I had that Cheshire was dirty, and only a fool would count on him.

I decided to give us a hole card.

Joe Vaster was not listed in the Miami white pages, but enough Vasters were that within three calls, a surly button man transferred me to a sleepy Joe Vaster.

I identified myself.

He interrupted me. "They tell me you want to talk to me about my boy. Then talk."

NINETEEN

NEXT MORNING JUST after nine, we pulled up to the curb in front of the Seaman's Center. "You sure we have time for this before the *California* comes in?" Virgil asked.

I climbed out of the pickup and glanced in the direction of the bay. "It isn't due until noon."

With a satisfied grunt, Virgil tagged along after me.

A dozen seamen were in the recreation room, some reading the local news, others shooting pool, a few gossiping. A potpourri of world cultures, they glanced up at us when we entered, then returned to their own business.

I picked out a loner who was thumbing through a worn copy of the National Enquirer. Dark-skinned, he appeared to be a Middle Easterner. "You speak English?"

He glanced up at me, then looked to his left and right as if reassuring himself I was speaking to him. "Some," he replied.

"You work on container vessels?" I nodded in the direction of the docks.

He stared blankly at us. Finally, he answered. "Some."

I grinned at Virgil and handed the dark-skinned man a slip of paper with the numbers 1-146-1-21 written on it. "These numbers mean anything to you?"

He frowned at the slip of paper, looked back up at me and shook his head. "Some."

"What?"

He stared at me blankly. "Some."

Virgil rolled his eyes.

I showed the numbers to the other seamen in the recreation room. A few could not speak English. Those that could were no help.

"So MUCH FOR the Seaman's Center," Virgil growled when we climbed back in my truck. "Sorry about that. It was a waste of time."

I started the engine and shrugged. "No. It was a shot. We could've hit it. Now we go to Plan B."

"Which is?" He looked at me skeptically.

"How many berths in the Port of Galveston?"

Virgil shrugged. "Beats me. Thirty or forty, probably."

"And how many do you figure handle container vessels? Or a better question still—how many berths do not handle containers?"

A gleam of understanding lit his eyes, then faded into a frown. "What if Abbandando spots us snooping around?"

I turned west on Avenue A and headed for 37th Avenue, which would take us into the westernmost piers on the dockside. "He won't."

We turned off on 37th and drove in front of berths 39,

40, and 41, which I guessed to be a mile or more from Abbandando's operation.

"The docks are all fenced in with guards." Virgil gestured toward the length of chain link fence stretching out of sight in both directions. "How we going to get inside?"

"We don't need to," I replied, pulling onto the shoulder near the fence separating us from berth 41. I pointed to the aluminum containers, ten feet wide, twelve high, and thirty long. They were stacked four high the entire width of the dock. "Take a look."

On each top corner of the container units was a set of numerals, similar to those I held in my hand. I read the first aloud. "4-6839-14-41"

Virgil grumbled. "That's more numbers than we got."

"Different shipper, but take a look. The last two digits on this one is the ship's berth, 41."

His eyes lit up. "Yeah. Like our number with the 21 at the end."

"Exactly. I'm guessing that each shipping line probably has its own identification code. What we're looking for back at Abbandando's is this particular combination," I explained, gesturing to the numbers in my hand.

He studied me a moment, considering my explanation. "In other words, we find the container with '1-146-1-21,' and that's it?"

I gave him a wistful grin and shook my head. "I sure hope so, Virge. I sure hope so."

WE SWUNG BY the motel to pick up the visitors' passes and overalls.

I failed to notice the little red Miata roadster in the parking lot when I dropped Virgil off to retrieve our passes and uniforms from my room. Had I seen the sports car, I wouldn't have parked. But I didn't, and I did.

You can imagine my surprise when I spotted Janice Coffman-Morrison, my on-again, off-again significant other, emerge from the lobby and wave energetically at me.

"Tony." She glanced at her diamond-encrusted watch. With her patented pout, she said, "I've been waiting for almost an hour. Where have you been?"

I stared at her, dumbfounded, remembering the last visit she'd paid me when she slapped me halfway back to Louisiana. Though wary of her intentions, I was happy to see her, although she was the last one I wanted to see today. I had too much going on to have Janice with me. I climbed out of the pickup to meet her. I stammered, then finally managed to blurt out a brilliant question. "What are you doing here?"

"Waiting for you, silly," she replied, smiling brightly.

I stepped back and raised my hand to my cheek in case she decided to come out swinging.

She laughed. "Oh, poor dear. I'm sorry about last time, Tony. I was so wrong." She looked around, spotted the restaurant. "Come on. I'm starving. Let's get something to eat, and I'll tell you all about it."

The brief exchange was pure Janice Coffman-Morrison,

little rich girl who always got whatever she wanted. But not this time. I grabbed her arm. "No. Not now, Janice."

She looked around at me in disbelief.

I led her toward my room. "I'll explain, but I've got two or three errands to run, and I can't put them off. I don't have the time."

At that moment, Virgil stepped out of my room, all decked out in his blue overalls and carrying the duffel bag with our gear. He frowned when he spotted Janice with me. "Here are the goods, Tony."

I nodded to the pickup. "Okay. Just—"

Janice interrupted. "Tony. What's going on? What do you mean you don't have time? Why, I—" She spotted the bag in Virgil's hand as he headed for the truck. "Who is that man, Tony? What is he carrying? He looks like a common laborer." She wrinkled her nose the way only a rich girl can.

"Look. I've got a couple of important errands. I can't put them off. I don't know how long it will take, but why don't you wait up in my room for me? We can go out for a nice dinner tonight."

A suspicious frown wrinkled her forehead. "Does my cousin have anything to do with this?"

It was neither the time nor place to reveal her cousin was not her cousin, but a fraud, so I did what any red-blooded man would do. I lied. "No."

Janice sniffed. "Well, I don't want to stay in your room. I came here so you could take me to see Ted."

"Morrison? I thought you saw him a few days ago."

With a brief shrug, she replied. "Oh, he wasn't home. I figured you could take me to see him and then we all could go out to eat."

I shook my head. "This isn't a good time, Janice."

"Why not?"

"Errands. I have important errands to run."

She pursed her lips in a pout. "Well, then take me with you."

That was the last thing I needed. "I wish you would wait here for me."

"No. I want to go with you." She gave me the look.

I didn't have a choice. If I wanted to get to the docks in time, I'd have to take her with me. Shaking my head in frustration, I grabbed her arm and dragged her after me. "Then come on. But stay out of the way, and don't be asking a bunch of questions."

She pulled up when she saw my old pickup. "Not that truck, Tony. You know I can't stand riding in that truck."

"My room or the truck," I said with finality, opening the driver's door.

Inside, Virgil gaped at us.

I rolled my eyes at him. "My girlfriend," I said by way of explanation.

"But Tony—"

"Forget it, Virge. She's going with us." I glared at her. "But she's staying in the pickup."

She arched an eyebrow in protest.

I added. "Otherwise, it's my room."

Her shoulders sagged. "All right." The resignation in

her voice brightened when she added, "But you've got to tell me what this is all about."

Virgil groaned.

I climbed into my overalls and started the pickup. "You got everything, Virge?"

He nodded and rolled his eyes. "Yeah. Right here." He patted the black duffel bag on his lap.

MY PLAN WAS SIMPLE. Virgil and I would stake out the *California* as soon as it berthed at 21. We each had our cell phones so we could stay in touch. Our can of paint was in the duffel bag.

If Morrison didn't make a move, then we'd have to wait for Abbandando. Even if we discovered the container with the shipment of British Paint, we wouldn't know which can contained the diamonds.

As we made our way through the traffic toward the docks, I glanced down at Janice. She wore her usual upscale clothes: a long leather coat, a green dress that screamed "expensive," and high heels. Not ideal apparel for the Galveston docks, but then she was remaining in the truck.

We pulled into a parking lot outside the gates. Virgil handed me a pair of binoculars.

I pointed a finger at Janice. "Remember. Stay in the truck. The keys are in it if you get cold."

I could see flickers of defiance in her eyes, but she nodded. "How long will you be gone?"

Virgil shrugged when I looked at him. "I don't know. Just you stay put. You hear?"

She nodded briefly, too briefly, I later decided. I should have known, but we had no choice. To paraphrase an old saying, time and smuggled diamonds wait for no one.

As we departed the truck, Virgil growled, "I got a bad feeling about her, Tony."

I slung the duffel bag over my shoulder. "Believe me, Virge, it was either bring her or stay at the motel. Trust me, she won't be a problem. Don't worry." I don't know who I was trying to convince, Virgil or myself.

LUCKILY FOR US, security at the docks was slack. With our visitors' passes fastened to our jackets, Virgil and I strolled through the gates and crossed a hundred yards of concrete, where we leaped aboard a slow-moving train for berth 21.

Suddenly, Virgil hit me on the shoulder. "Tony! Look. Both ships."

I gaped in surprise.

Tugboats were slowly easing the *California*, a 285-foot, 2,700-ton cargo vessel, up the channel. A few hundred yards behind was the *Voyager*, being eased forward into the port.

I shot Virgil a look of disbelief. "The *Voyager* wasn't due for another two or three days."

He shook his head. "Maybe not, but whether we like it or not, we got it."

194 GALVESTON

We leaped from the train and watched as the tugs slipped the *California* into berth 23. At the same time, the *Voyager* docked at berth 21. I caught my breath when I spotted the containers on the deck of the ship. Through the binoculars, I counted twenty containers on the *Voyager* and twenty-six on the *California*. I couldn't discern the numbers on them, but the configuration was the same as the set we discovered in Albert Vaster's apartment.

"Okay, Virge. You take the *California*. I'll watch the *Voyager*. Stay in touch."

He nodded, checking his cell phone. "I got a full battery."

We split up. I took my place on a catwalk leading up to an idle shore crane near berth 21. Virgil made his way to berth 23.

One moment, the pier was deserted, the next it bustled with activity. Stevedores from Maritime Shippers swarmed over the vessel like crabs on a dead fish. Gantry cranes whined into motion, dropping thick strands of steel down to the deck while men swarmed to hook them to the giant containers.

One by one, the containers were moved from the deck to a loading zone where they were stacked in neat rows. I called Virgil. "You make out the numbers on the containers?"

"Yeah. But ain't seen the one we're looking for. These are all 21 down here, too."

By now, the last container had been removed from

the deck and the holds unsecured, revealing three huge black squares opening into the bowels of the vessel.

Engines whining, three great shore cranes swung their arms around, dropping lines into the respective holds. Pallet loads of cargo were slowly off-loaded from two of the holds onto waiting trucks and rail cars. The third hold held more containers.

I glanced over my shoulder in the direction of my pickup. I couldn't see Janice inside. I hoped she had decided to take a nap, but a sinking feeling in my stomach told me differently. I shook my head. I thought the world of her, but she could be mighty stubborn at times.

Suddenly, a bright yellow container leaped out at me from the hold of the *Voyager*.

I slapped the binoculars to my eyes. On the side of the yellow container was the bright green logo of a paintbrush. At that moment, my phone jangled. "Yeah, Virge. What's up?"

"He's here, Tony. He's here. I tell you, I saw him."

"Hold on, Virge. Who? Calm down. Who are you talking about?"

He hesitated. "I'm not sure. It doesn't look like Morrison. Morrison is blond. This one has black hair, but he just came down the gangplank. He's wearing red overalls, and he's carrying a yellow can in his hand."

"What?"

"You heard me."

"It can't be. I'm staring at the container of British Paint now. This has to be the one."

"I don't care. There's some guy here, and he's carrying a yellow can in his hand."

I jammed the binoculars to my eyes. I couldn't spot our man, but berth 23 was three hundred yards distant. I groaned. Why did everything have to be so difficult?

"You sure it isn't Morrison?"

"He's wearing a cap and sunglasses. And he's got a limp. I don't know who it is, but he's carrying a can of the paint."

TWENTY

I GLANCED AT the yellow container being lowered to the ground. Hastily, I tore my eyes away and leaned as far over the railing as I dared while scanning the bustle of activity at berth 23 with my binoculars. "Where is he, Virge?" I yelled into my cell phone. "I don't see him."

"He's just now reaching the bow of the ship. Looks like he's cutting across berth 22 heading for Abbandando's warehouse."

Abbandando's? One of the fat man's boys? Had to be. I thought fast. I had to reach him before he entered the warehouse. Once inside, we were sunk. He'd take the diamonds straight to Pete. "Keep me posted of his location, Virge. I'm coming down to try to catch up to him before he gets to the warehouse."

I clambered down the stairs to the dock, at the same time trying to keep my eyes on our man. Suddenly, a familiar voice froze me in place.

"Tony. Where are you going now?"

I looked around at Janice, who was standing at the base of the stairs looking up at me.

"I was bored," she said. "Let's go. We've been here over an hour."

Virgil's voice crackled over the cell phone. "Hurry up, Tony. He's getting closer."

There was no time to explain anything to her, so I grabbed Janice by the arm and dragged her after me. "Then come on. We don't have time to waste."

"But…" She stumbled, caught her balance, and fell in behind me, her high heels click, click, clicking on the dock. "What's the hurry?"

Ignoring her, I spoke into the small phone. "You still see him, Virge?"

"Yeah, but he's getting closer. I'm after him."

Janice yanked on my hand. "Tony. Stop. What's going on?"

"I'll tell you later. Now come on." Ahead of me, empty freight cars awaited loading on the tracks in a long curve. Out of sight around the curve of freight cars was the entrance to Abbandando's warehouse.

Suddenly, Virgil exclaimed, "Look out, Tony! He's heading in your direction. Along the tracks."

I jerked to a halt. I looked around, guessing I probably had less than thirty seconds before our boy rounded the curve in the tracks. If he spotted me, no telling what he would do.

We were standing beside the open doors of an empty freight car. I tossed the duffel bag inside, grabbed Janice by the waist and set her on the threshold, and hoisted myself inside.

"Tony, what—"

I held my finger to her lips. "Hush. Back here," I

whispered, grabbing the duffel bag and hurrying her to the rear of the car. "I'll explain later," I whispered. "Wait here."

Before she could protest, I crept to the edge of the open door and peered outside. The uniform-clad stevedore limped around the outer curve of the track, then cut diagonally across the dock toward the open warehouse door.

He had me puzzled. Was this black-haired guy one of Abbandando's, or had Morrison taken a partner?

I surveyed the area. The only hiding spot was a maintenance vehicle halfway between me and the warehouse.

I had one chance, one very slim chance. If I could make the vehicle without the courier spotting me, maybe I could get to him before he reached the warehouse.

I caught a movement from the corner of my eye. It was Virgil. He had rounded the curve, then ducked back.

We both held our breath and watched as the courier grew even with the parked maintenance vehicle. Abruptly, he halted, glanced around, then slowly limped to the pickup and deposited the can in the pickup bed.

Straightening, he scanned the area once again, brushed his hands together in satisfaction, then headed back toward the train. I stepped back, just enough so I could keep him in sight, but not so much that he could spot me back in the darkness of the empty car. To my surprise, his limp vanished. That's when I became suspicious.

I frowned. What was he up to? Another goombah

double-crossing someone? He couldn't have been one of Abbandando's. I shrugged. I wasn't going to worry about unraveling all the confusion. All I wanted was that can of diamonds.

When the thief disappeared from sight, I unzipped the duffel bag and retrieved the yellow can of British Paint. Time for Plan B, or C, or whatever we were up to at this point.

After warning Janice to stay back in the shadows of the car, I paused in the open doorway of the freight car, scanned the dock quickly, then leaped to the ground. My heart thudded in my chest. Less than a hundred yards away was a fortune in smuggled diamonds, just waiting for me.

Suddenly, it hit me that the diamonds were indeed worth millions. Millions! And why did I want them? To prove Frank Cheshire and District Attorney George Briggs were dirty in an effort to clear me of the shooting of Ben Howard.

On the other hand, if I had millions, why should I even worry about Cheshire and Briggs and Howard? Greed reared its ugly head.

I stumbled on the concrete and fell to my knees, tearing a hole in the knee of my overalls. My can of paint rolled a few feet before I grabbed it. I glanced around the dock hurriedly, hoping my fall had drawn no notice. Why had I ever paid Ben a visit to begin with? I would have been better off returning to Austin and my one exotic fish, the little brain-damaged albino tiger barb, Oscar.

Before I realized it, I was standing at the side of the maintenance vehicle, a white Chevrolet C-250. I looked into the bed. A dozen or so cans of paint were jammed into a corner.

I lifted my can of paint over the side of the pickup. Before I could make the switch, a squeal of tires jerked my attention away from the paint. I looked up to see a Lincoln Town Car racing out of Abbandando's warehouse and heading directly for me, smoke boiling up from the rear tires.

I could say that with cool aplomb, I simply turned and walked casually toward the freight cars, but the truth is, I panicked and ran, the yellow British Paint can swinging wildly in my hand.

Naturally, the Town Car intercepted me before I reached the train. I stood staring at the rolled-up black windows. I remember thinking they were blacker than midnight down on a Louisiana bayou.

With a soft hum, the rear window eased down. "Mustache Pete" Abbandando waved a clean-picked barbecued rib at me, its grease plastering his thin mustache to his fat lips. He nodded. "Hello, Tony. Going somewhere?" He glanced at the yellow can in my hand and dragged the tip of his tongue across his mustache.

I figured I was about two seconds away from entertaining a dozen slugs from an AK-47. "Not really, Pete.

Just taking a stroll along the docks. Foreign ships always fascinated me." I rolled my eyes at my own idiocy.

He nodded to the can. "You planning on going somewhere with my property?"

I gaped at him for a moment, unable to believe my ears. Was the impossible so likely? Did he really think I had grabbed the can Morrison had placed in the bed of the pickup? With eyes wide open and a childlike innocence spread over my face, I replied, "Your property, Pete?" I held up the can of British Paint. "This can of paint? This is yours?"

The passenger door popped open, and a nattily dressed thug lumbered out. He scowled down at me.

I looked at Pete, who simply nodded. "You're a good boy, Tony. Don't get hurt. Not yet. Give Crusher the can of paint."

Taking a deep breath, I played at being reluctant, but under Crusher's glowering stare, not too reluctant.

"Mustache Pete" broke the tense silence. "Don't be no hero, Tony. My experience is that heroes usually get hurt bad."

I gave Pete a lopsided grin. "Heroes don't run on my side of the family, Pete. Here." I offered Crusher the can. I shivered when I saw the disappointment on the big man's face upon my so willingly giving up the can of paint. "Sorry to disappoint you, Crusher."

"Huh?" His overhanging eyebrows and broad forehead wrinkled in a frown. "Huh?" His frown deepened.

I saw right then that whimsical sarcasm was not Crusher's forte.

"Take the can, Crusher," Pete said, a touch of impatience edging his greasy voice.

Towering over me, Crusher took the paint. I had the distinct feeling he would have no problem crushing the gallon can in one hand and my throat in the other.

I took a step back, trying to stay in the loser role Pete pinned on me. "Now what? Joe Vaster is going to be upset."

Pete leered at me, his thick, fat lips turning inside out, hiding the thin mustache below his flaring nostrils. "What can I say, Tony? Poor old Sam Maranzano will help us out on this."

I looked around. I couldn't see Virgil or Janice, who, for once, must have done as I asked and remained in the freight car.

Pete arched an eyebrow at Crusher, who then obediently shook the can. Glass rattled inside. A smug grin replaced the leer on Pete's porky face. At Pete's nod, Crusher set the can on the floorboard in front of the shotgun seat of the Town Car.

I stilled the anticipation boiling my blood. What should I do when Pete drove away? Go immediately to the can of diamonds still in the bed of the pickup? Leave them until later? Call the police?

With a grunt, Pete slid to the far side of the rear seat. His command cut off the plans I was laying. "Now, Tony. Climb in."

"Huh?"

He patted the seat at his side. "Here. We're going for a trip."

I took a backward step. "I don't think so, Pete. I have backup out here."

He laughed, the old Richard Widmark sneer. "You mean them two?"

I looked around to see two goons marching Janice and Virgil toward us. I groaned.

Without warning, my head snapped back as a powerful blow struck me in the middle of the back, slamming me toward the open door of the Town Car. "Mister Abbandando, he say inside." Crusher growled. "Now!"

Reacting impulsively, I spun and swung a wild right at Crusher, who simply grabbed my fist and leered at me. "You want me to hurt him, Mister Abbandando?"

"No, Crusher. Not yet."

I made a wild stab at bluffing my way out. "People know I'm here, Pete. They'll find my pickup and ask questions."

He half snorted, half chuckled. "In five minutes, that piece of junk you call a pickup will be a three-by-three square of metal on the way to the foundry."

To HIS CREDIT, "Mustache Pete" didn't immediately measure us for cement shoes. Instead, he marched us to the elevator and whisked us up to the fourth floor.

A custodian in dark blue overalls with MARITIME SHIPPERS blazed across the back and wearing a billed cap

perched on one side of his bald head was busy sweeping up trash. I just caught a glimpse of him. He looked
strangely familiar, but I didn't have time to wonder about
him. They shoved us into a storage room that had been
converted to a lounge and left two goons to watch us.

Shelves containing janitorial and toilet items lined
two walls. A small TV sat on a table next to a refrigerator along the third wall. The couch on which they
shoved the three of us took up the fourth wall. A door
beside one of the shelves opened into a tiny bathroom
with a small window.

"Sit. And keep your yaps closed."

The two button men took the straightback chairs on
either side of the room, about halfway between us and
the TV. Each sat stiff-backed, glaring at us and resting a
short-barreled blue revolver in his lap. Part of the frame
was shiny where the serial number had been filed off.
The grips were wrapped with tape. Hit pieces. Designed
for a onetime use, then dumped.

For the first few minutes, we remained silent. I wondered if we were scheduled for the one-time use of the
snub-nosed revolvers.

Fortunately, a Road Runner cartoon was on, challeng-
ing our guards' intellectual capabilities. The two goons
were torn between keeping an eye on us and guffawing
at the misfortune of Wile E. Coyote.

The blasting of the TV and the cackling of our guards
covered our whispers. "What are they going to do with
us?" Janice glanced at them fearfully.

Virgil arched an eyebrow. I whispered back, "I don't know, but we can't afford to wait around and find out."

I searched the room for weapons. All I saw on the metal shelves were rolls of toilet paper, stacks of white disinfectant cakes for commodes and urinals, brown rolls of paper towels, and cans of air fresheners. Not much against two handguns.

One of the guards laughed, his attention focused on Wile E. Coyote falling into an almost bottomless canyon, followed by a boulder the size of the *Queen Mary*.

That's when I looked again at the shelves lining the walls. A surge of hope caught in my throat. The shelves were free standing. While they wouldn't carry the impact of a Queen Mary, loaded as they were, they could provide enough confusion for us to get the jump on the two goons—maybe.

I caught Virgil's attention, then nodded to the shelves.

He frowned.

I eyed the top of the shelf behind the nearest thug, then pointed at the ground with a finger.

His eyes lit in momentary understanding before his lips mouthed the word "How?"

Rubbing my hands together, I nodded to the bathroom.

A faint smile ticked up the edge of his lips.

I called to the guard nearest us, "Hey. I need to use the john."

The other one growled, "You stay where you are, buddy. Nobody moves."

I shook my head. "You'll be sorry."

The second one interrupted. "Go ahead. I can watch him from here, Sid. No sweat." He jerked his head toward the bathroom. "I said go ahead. And leave the door open," he added.

"Watch'm good, Mert."

Mert watched until I started washing my hands. I suppose that wasn't as intellectually stimulating as the cartoons, as he turned back to the Road Runner and Wile E. Coyote.

Virgil and I locked eyes as I started from the bathroom.

Just before I reached for the shelves, the door burst open, ripped from its hinges. All I spotted was a figure wearing sunglasses leaping through. I thought I saw his hair fly off, but I was too busy yanking the shelves over onto Mert, who was still in his chair. The impact knocked him over backward to the floor, covering him with rolls of toilet paper.

I followed the paper, landing on the shelves and slamming the edge of a shelf into the bridge of his nose. He cried out. Blindly, his fist shot up through the tumble of toilet paper rolls, just grazing my jaw.

All I could see of Mert beneath the rolls of toilet tissue and urinal cakes were his arms flailing wildly between the metal shelves that still lay on top of him. I did the best I could, slamming my own fists into the rolls of tissue just about where I thought his head was.

Suddenly, I hit something hard. I couldn't tell if it was the metal shelf or Mert, but I hit it again.

I must have been hitting Mert, because his flailing arms stiffened, then dropped limply to the pile of toilet tissue.

Just as I looked up, a gunshot boomed, followed by a curse, and then an excited voice yelling, "Take this, and this, and this."

I was surprised to see Ted Morrison straddling Sid, pummeling him unmercifully as the thug vainly tried to ward off the blows.

Rolling off the rack of shelves, I scrabbled about for Mert's revolver, fumbled with it, then stumbled to my feet and yelled at Abbandando's two goons. "Back off! Get your hands up!"

Virgil lay groaning a few feet away. Janice knelt at his side.

Morrison jerked his head around in alarm, but when he saw me holding the revolver, he closed his eyes and sighed with relief.

The second revolver had flown from Sid's hand when the door slammed into him and had landed against the far wall. I retrieved it and jammed it under my belt.

The thug beneath Morrison groaned. Morrison grabbed him by the lapels and drew back his fist.

"That's enough, Morrison," I shouted. "He's had enough."

Janice looked up and her eyes grew wide when she

saw Morrison. "Ted. What— What are you doing here?" She looked at me, confused. "Tony, what's going on?"

Still clutching Sid by the lapels, Morrison looked up, his fist poised for another blow. He didn't recognize Janice. He looked at me.

That's when I noticed he was wearing red overalls. I shook my head. "I said that's enough. Let him go."

He nodded and leaned back, releasing the unconscious goon's lapels and letting his head bounce off the floor.

With a shaky laugh, I muttered, "I'm glad you dropped in when you did."

Agitated, he glanced around the room. "Where's Abbandando?"

"What do you mean?"

Morrison spun on me, his face twisted in anger. "I saw you running with the diamonds before Abbandando stopped you. I thought he was up here with you."

Janice hurried to him. "Ted, are you all right?"

He stared at her. "Yeah. Yeah. I'm fine." He hesitated, glanced at me, then back to Janice. "Who are you?"

Janice pressed her hand to her lips in shock. She looked at me in disbelief.

I didn't know what else to say except, "Ted, this is your cousin, Janice Coffman-Morrison."

TWENTY-ONE

HE STARED AT HER for several seconds before looking back at me. "You didn't tell her?"

His question jarred Janice from her stunned shock. "Tell me…"

"No." I shook my head. "There hasn't been time."

"Tell me what?" Her tone became more demanding. She shook my arm. "Tony. Tell me what?"

Before I could reply, the sound of sirens and screeching tires filled the air. I hurried to the bathroom window and peered down at the dock. My blood ran cold. Sergeant Jim Wilson was at the head of a squad of armed cops and they were racing into the warehouse.

"Who is it?" Morrison called out.

I couldn't help glaring at him suspiciously. "Your buddy, Wilson. Sergeant Jim Wilson."

He gave me a puzzled look. "Wilson? I don't know any Wilson."

Janice called from the other room, "Tony, hurry! Your friend needs a doctor. He's bleeding bad."

I jammed the revolver in my pocket and muttered a curse. I had no choice but to believe him. "Come on, Morrison. Help me get him out of here."

He hesitated.

With a shrug, I said, "Abbandando and the diamonds are long gone, Morrison. Forget them." It was a small lie, worth only, say, about thirty million or so. As soon as I told it, my conscience started nagging at me. I did my best to ignore it.

He studied me a moment, shook his head in disgust, and reached for Virgil.

We hoisted him between us, his arms over our shoulders. Janice led the way to the elevator. I called to her, "The stairs. They'll be watching the elevator."

She glanced over her shoulder and frowned. "And not the stairs?" She continued toward the stairway.

Beyond the stairs, another one hundred feet, I spotted a sign reading, "Emergency exit." I nodded to it. "That one. Take the emergency exit. Maybe they'll overlook it."

Just as we reached the door, the elevator bell chimed behind us. We jerked open the emergency exit and slammed the door as racing footsteps echoed down the hall.

Virgil was a dead weight. We stumbled down the stairs with him. Between clenched teeth, I muttered to Morrison, "You don't know Wilson? He's in thick with Abbandando and Briggs."

Morrison shot a glance at me. "I never heard Cheshire say nothing about a dirty cop by that name."

Virgil groaned.

Janice stayed half a floor ahead of us, signaling us at each level to continue. Finally, we reached the ground floor.

Pausing to catch my breath, I stared at the closed door. My conscience got the better of me. "If I'm not mistaken, this door opens onto the dock. The pickup you put the diamonds in is no more than a hundred feet away. I didn't—"

"I know. I saw Abbandando take them from you."

Morrison had interrupted me before I could tell him the truth, which I quickly decided was a sign that Fate wanted me to keep the secret to myself.

"Diamonds!" Janice's jaw dropped open. "What diamonds?"

I nodded to the door. "Time enough for that later. Open the door, and let's go."

She flung open the door, and we froze.

Glaring at us with drawn revolvers and cold resolve in their eyes were six Galveston cops with Sergeant Jim Wilson at their head.

When he saw me, the grim frown on his face faded, replaced with a broad grin. "Am I glad to see you, Boudreaux. I thought we were too late." He gestured to a couple of his men. "Adams, Wolfe, get these people to the squad car. You others get inside. Find Abbandando and Briggs."

If Wilson's reception hadn't confused me enough, his orders sent my head spinning. Before I could put together any kind of question, the two officers hustled us to a cruiser.

So much had happened so quickly that I didn't even have time to think about the diamonds during our rush to the hospital. Once there, we carried Virgil to the emergency room where doctors and nurses hustled us out and turned back to their patient.

The three of us, Janice, Morrison, and me, found ourselves in the waiting room staring at each other. The two uniforms, Wolfe and Adams, stood just outside the door, making sure we waited for Sergeant Wilson.

I wasn't sure if I should tell Wilson about the diamonds or not. What if someone stumbled across them? But who? I glanced at the closed door, anxiously awaiting Wilson's return.

I tried to put the events of the last few days in perspective, but regardless of the storyboard I drew, it had a dozen empty holes and incidents for which there was no explanation.

The reason Morrison had returned was obvious: the diamonds. But why had Wilson saved us? What did he mean by sending the cops after Abbandando and Briggs? Why had he earlier been trying to find Morrison?

Janice broke into the turmoil tumbling about in my skull. "What diamonds were you two talking about, Tony?"

Turning to Morrison, I said, "Maybe you better explain it. You're the one who put them in the pickup."

He grinned sheepishly. "You had me figured out, huh?"

"Yeah. For someone who was planning on leaving town, you waited around a spell."

He ducked his head. "Now, Tony. I didn't exactly tell you when I was leaving, just that I was going." He shrugged and shot a furtive glance at the two cops at the door. "I don't see any way out of here right now. Abbandando'll probably be gone when we get back, just like you said. Him and the diamonds."

I shrugged nonchalantly. "Probably."

Janice exclaimed in frustration, "Will one of you tell me about the diamonds? Ted? You know about them? It's obvious Tony won't tell me."

Morrison studied me a moment. "Why not? And there are one or two other things you need to know, Miss Coffman."

"Miss Coffman?" A puzzled frown wrinkled Janice's forehead. "Is this some kind of joke, Ted?"

"No, ma'am. It isn't. And I'm not your cousin."

Her eyes widened in disbelief as Morrison told his story about the DNA deception and the smuggled diamonds. "Truth is, I didn't care about you or your aunt. It was just a hustle. I figured on picking up a few hundred thousand, but that was before my hustling just about got me measured for a six-foot-deep hole. Then I wanted out. That's why I told Tony about you and the DNA business. I just want a clean break." He gave me a crooked grin. "Truth is, I'm glad the diamonds are gone. Who needs them? I figure I can make a good living selling used cars."

I was feeling pretty good about then.

Janice stared at him in shock for several seconds. Slowly, she turned to me. "Why didn't you tell me, Tony?"

I closed my eyes and leaned back on the couch, suppressing my laughter.

"I don't see what's so funny."

Leaning forward, I laid my hand on hers. "This morning at the motel was the first time I've seen you since Morrison, or whatever his name is, told me the truth. We've been pretty busy since then, too busy to sit and chat."

"But—"

At that moment, Sergeant Jim Wilson entered. He stopped when he saw me and nodded. "Well, Boudreaux. It's all wrapped up. We got Abbandando and Briggs on the run. We busted their little organization into a hundred pieces."

I eyed him warily. "Briggs? But, I thought you... You're not part... I thought that you and Briggs... Well..." My words faded away.

He shrugged. "I had to keep you off balance. Your exploits, for better or for worse, caused Briggs to get careless. He was afraid those good old boys he'd been taking bribes from would get cold feet and back out, so he and Abbandando planned to get rid of you like they did Albert Vaster. We have it all on tape, and right now, all of their records are being confiscated." He chuckled. "I imagine there will be more than one CEO who is going to have quite a headache tomorrow."

I gestured to Morrison. "Off balance, huh? Is that why you called me at the motel looking for him?"

"No. Briggs didn't know about him. I'd got word

some of the meateaters on the force were after Morrison. I wanted to put him where he wouldn't be hurt. I'd been sent in here by the Attorney General in Austin three years ago to nail Briggs and his bunch. We knew Briggs and Abbandando were bedmates, but it took your fumbling around to force them to make their mistakes."

His assessment of my achievements wasn't any too flattering. "But you were my informant."

He grinned sheepishly. "Sorry for lying, but I couldn't take a chance on you talking to the wrong person."

I frowned. "What about the first call? The one saying Cheshire was in the smuggling caper with Maranzano?"

Wilson shook his head. "Not me. From the phone records, it looks like it was Briggs. Obviously, he was trying to shift your investigation to Maranzano."

"So then it was Briggs who sent those goons after me. The drive-by, the mugs on the dock, even the shooter at the cement company. All were sent by Briggs."

Wilson arched an eyebrow. "And Abbandando. He was the one who sent you a bodyguard. That bothered us at first until we found out it was Virgil." He cleared his throat. "Nobody buys Virgil. He's one of us we sent in here a couple years back."

I shook my head in wonder. "How'd you find us at the warehouse?"

He chuckled. "Well, my contacts were keeping an eye on you, but we lost you. Maranzano tipped us to your situation."

"Maranzano?" It was my turn to stare in disbelief.

Wilson nodded. "Yeah. Seems like he got a call from Joe Vaster to keep an eye on you. Apparently, when Mister Vaster talks, Sam Maranzano listens."

"Joe Vaster?" I grinned crookedly. He worked fast. I'd only spoken to him a few hours earlier.

"One of his boys worked for Maranzano. A bald-headed goombah. Joe put him there to keep his eyes on Sam. He was the one who passed the word."

Then I remembered the bald-headed goon in Maranzano's office, the same bald-headed guy who was sweeping the floor at Abbandando's warehouse when they hustled us into the fourth-floor storeroom. I shrugged. "That was nice of him."

Wilson grinned crookedly. "You got an odd collection of friends, Boudreaux."

"Yeah. Must be my charm. By the way," I added, changing the subject. "What's going to happen to Abbandando and Briggs now that they're in custody?"

He shook his head, his face quickly growing somber. "We don't have 'em. They slipped through our fingers, but we'll get them. Unless Joe Vaster gets them first. If they're smart, they'll come to us instead of facing Vaster." He paused. "I heard you told Vaster where he could find his son."

"Yeah. There were too many coincidences—the fresh cement, the shoe print, the single wingtip shoe."

"What gave you a clue?"

"When I told Abbandando what had taken place that night, he asked about the cement truck and the running feet. I didn't think about it until later. That's when I realized I'd never mentioned the truck or the running feet to him. They only way he could have known was from one of his boys, which meant he had to know what was going on."

Wilson breathed out deeply. "Not bad. Actually, you did a pretty fair job. Well, you don't have to worry now. You're off the hook. We've got enough on Abbandando and Briggs to keep them off the streets for ninety years. Besides, Ben Howard came out of his coma an hour ago."

I felt a hundred pounds lighter.

Janice squeezed my hand. "Oh, Tony. That's wonderful, wonderful."

Wilson glanced at the door. He extended his hand to me and winked. "Well, Boudreaux, truth is, you're okay. A little green, but you're learning. If you get tired of the P.I. work, come see me."

I took his hand. "Thanks." I glanced at Morrison, who was eyeing me warily. Both of us realized Wilson had said nothing about the diamonds. Maybe he didn't even know about them.

WE VISITED VIRGIL in his room. He was still groggy from the anesthesia, but he promised to visit me in Austin one day if I would make him a Louisiana gumbo. I agreed.

Ben Howard was less generous, making me promise never to come back to visit him. "You're nothing but trouble, Boudreaux," he added with a big wink and hearty handshake. "But, at least, you're my trouble."

Janice didn't understand our exchange, but I did. It was a man's way of saying "I'll see you later."

As ABBANDANDO HAD PROMISED, my pickup had turned into a three-foot square of metal, so Morrison, Janice, and I rode back to the motel in a police cruiser.

Two or three times during the ride, Morrison and I exchanged glances. Both of us were well aware no one had asked questions about the diamonds.

Morrison peered out the side window. "I wonder where Abbandando is?"

"Beats me," I replied with a shrug, knowing full well he was wondering about the diamonds, trying to cook up some scheme to snatch them from the fat man.

We said nothing, each consumed with sordid emotions of greed.

Our bald-headed friend was waiting at my door for us.

He nodded to Janice and gave us a sheepish grin. "Mister Vaster wants to thank you for your assistance." He handed me a keychain with two keys. He pointed to a bright red Chevrolet Silverado pickup in the parking lot.

"Th…thanks," I stammered and stuttered, but I took the keys. I told myself I was taking the keys just to humor Mister Vaster, but I knew better. I had been salivating over those Silverados for the last couple years.

Bald-head's demeanor shifted from meek to menacing although the smile remained on his face. "Mister Vaster would also like to have his goods."

I looked at Morrison.

For a moment, we stared at each other. Then with a sheepish grin, I turned back to our visitor. Clearing my throat, I said, "No problem. Outside the main entrance to Abbandando's warehouse is a maintenance pickup."

"And—"

I gave him the details.

When I finished, he made a call on his cell phone.

Morrison just stared at me in disbelief. "You mean, all the time, you knew—"

"I was going to tell you. Honest."

He nodded slowly. "Oh, yeah. I bet you were."

Five minutes later, the phone rang. Our visitor answered, listened, nodded, punched off the phone, and looked up at me.

A big grin played over his lips. "Mister Vaster thanks you—for his goods and his son."

That's when I was glad I had not mentioned the diamonds to Sergeant Wilson.

Morrison shook his head. "Some people, you just can't trust."

I nodded. "Ain't it the truth."

We grinned at each other.

ONE GOOD THING that came out of it all was that Janice didn't mind riding in my new Silverado. In fact, we towed her Miata behind us back to Austin. We took the scenic route around by San Antonio then up to the springs at San Marcos.

I lost money on my little side trip to Galveston. By the time I paid the motel room, meals, and incidentals, plus a hefty bill from my attorney and IRS taxes on the pickup, I had eviscerated my bank account. I barely had enough to food for my albino tiger barb, Oscar.

But when I said goodbye to my friend Ben Howard in the hospital, the grin on his face was worth every cent. After all, good friends, regardless how grumpy and short-tempered, are few and far between.

* * * * *

REQUEST YOUR FREE BOOKS!

2 FREE NOVELS
PLUS 2 FREE GIFTS!

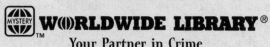

WORLDWIDE LIBRARY®

Your Partner in Crime

YES! Please send me 2 FREE novels from the Worldwide Library® series and my 2 FREE gifts (gifts are worth about $10). After receiving them, if I don't wish to receive any more books, I can return the shipping statement marked "cancel." If I don't cancel, I will receive 4 brand-new novels every month and be billed just $5.49 per book in the U.S. or $6.24 per book in Canada. That's a savings of at least 31% off the cover price. It's quite a bargain! Shipping and handling is just 50¢ per book in the U.S. and 75¢ per book in Canada.* I understand that accepting the 2 free books and gifts places me under no obligation to buy anything. I can always return a shipment and cancel at any time. Even if I never buy another book, the two free books and gifts are mine to keep forever.

414/424 WDN F4WY

Name	(PLEASE PRINT)	
Address		Apt. #
City	State/Prov.	Zip/Postal Code

Signature (if under 18, a parent or guardian must sign)

Mail to the Harlequin® Reader Service:
IN U.S.A.: P.O. Box 1867, Buffalo, NY 14240-1867
IN CANADA: P.O. Box 609, Fort Erie, Ontario L2A 5X3

Want to try two free books from another line?
Call 1-800-873-8635 or visit www.ReaderService.com.

* Terms and prices subject to change without notice. Prices do not include applicable taxes. Sales tax applicable in N.Y. Canadian residents will be charged applicable taxes. Offer not valid in Quebec. This offer is limited to one order per household. Not valid for current subscribers to the Worldwide Library series. All orders subject to credit approval. Credit or debit balances in a customer's account(s) may be offset by any other outstanding balance owed by or to the customer. Please allow 4 to 6 weeks for delivery. Offer available while quantities last.

Your Privacy—The Harlequin® Reader Service is committed to protecting your privacy. Our Privacy Policy is available online at www.ReaderService.com or upon request from the Harlequin Reader Service.

We make a portion of our mailing list available to reputable third parties that offer products we believe may interest you. If you prefer that we not exchange your name with third parties, or if you wish to clarify or modify your communication preferences, please visit us at www.ReaderService.com/consumerschoice or write to us at Harlequin Reader Service Preference Service, P.O. Box 9062, Buffalo, NY 14269. Include your complete name and address.

WWL13R

ReaderService.com

Manage your account online!

- Review your order history
- Manage your payments
- Update your address

> **We've designed
> the Harlequin® Reader Service
> website just for you.**

Enjoy all the features!

- Reader excerpts from any series
- Respond to mailings and special monthly offers
- Discover new series available to you
- Browse the Bonus Bucks catalog
- Share your feedback

Visit us at:
ReaderService.com

RS13